Santa Maybe

THE DUCHESS HOTEL #1

CARLA LUNA

MOON MANOR PRESS

First paperback edition: November 2024

Cover Design: *Bailey McGinn*
Editing: *Free Bird Editing*
Proofreading: *One Love Editing*

ISBN: 979-8-9894130-4-1 (paperback)
ISBN: 979-8-9894130-3-4 (ebook)

Published by Moon Manor Press
www.carlalunabooks.com

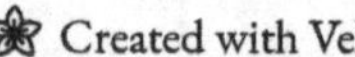 Created with Vellum

Author's Note

For those of you who might be unfamiliar with Canadian geography, *Santa Maybe* takes place in the beautiful city of Victoria, which is the provincial capital of British Columbia. It's located on the West Coast of Canada, on the southernmost tip of Vancouver Island (not to be confused with the city of Vancouver, which is on the mainland).

One of the reasons I set the Duchess Hotel series in Victoria is because I spent seventeen years of my life there, and I love going back to visit. The other reason is that the city is very popular with tourists, hence the competitive hotel market. Please note that in the interest of storytelling, I've taken a few liberties in my depiction of downtown Victoria, including the creation of two fictional hotels—the Duchess and the Grand Duke.

Content warning: while *Santa Maybe* is meant to provide an enjoyable Christmas romp, the book contains a character with toxic parents (who appear in the backstory and on the page) and a visit to a women's shelter for victims of domestic abuse.

One

53 *Days Until Christmas*

Rosie Gonzalez rarely left work before six. Or seven, if she was being honest. She didn't want anyone to think she was doing the bare minimum. But tonight, she wasn't staying a minute longer than she had to.

At exactly five thirty, she shut down her computer, grabbed her purse, and unpinned her shiny gold name badge from her blazer. As she set it beside her keyboard, she regarded it with a touch of pride: *Rosie Gonzalez—Assistant General Manager, The Duchess Hotel.*

Seconds later, her phone pinged with a text from the hotel's front office manager, Charlotte, who was known to her friends as Charlie. Rosie suspected she'd been counting down the minutes until tonight's happy hour.

> Charlie: Time for drinks at Pepe's! Duchess Damsels assemble!!

> Rosie: Yes!! Meet you in the lobby in 5.

She bit back a grin, eager for the salty-sweet tang of Pepe's irresistible house margaritas. Over the past two years, she and three of the hotel's managerial staff—the self-proclaimed "Duchess Damsels"—had made a habit of meeting up every other Friday to let off steam.

Another text appeared on her phone:

> Charlie: Just to warn you, Drew's meeting us at Pepe's.

Rosie's stomach fluttered with a sudden bout of nerves. She'd been looking forward to sharing drinks with her coworkers all day. But the prospect of seeing Drew Richardson changed everything. Ever since she'd paused her membership to Northlife Fitness last winter, she'd made a point of avoiding him.

Not that it was *his* fault.

Back when he'd been her personal trainer at the gym, they'd become friends. But she'd screwed up. First, she'd developed a huge crush on him, and then she'd lacked the confidence to tell him how she felt. Just as she'd been on the verge of confessing, he'd gotten involved with one of his coworkers. Which had sucked so much that Rosie had stopped going to the gym and lost touch with him.

> Rosie: Drew's coming? Why???

> Charlie: I thought you liked him. You used to talk about him all the time.

> Rosie: I did. But that was 8 months ago. Why now?

> Charlie: Ask Selena. She's the one who invited him.

Rosie let out a shaky breath. Why was she getting so worked up about this? In a few minutes, she'd have all the answers she needed.

When her desk phone rang, her shoulders tightened. *Please don't let it be an emergency.* Two nights ago, she'd stayed until eight, helping maintenance deal with a plumbing crisis on the third floor. When you worked at the oldest boutique hotel in Victoria, B.C., minor catastrophes like that were commonplace. It didn't help that the owners hadn't renovated the rooms in over twenty years.

To her dismay, the name Preston Hargreaves appeared on the caller ID.

Picking up the receiver, she greeted her boss with an enthusiasm she didn't feel. "Good evening, Mr. Hargreaves. Can I help you with something?"

"Sorry I had to postpone your employee review this morning, but I can finally fit you in. You're not on your way out yet, are you?"

Seriously? She'd spent all day waiting for that damn review.

"It'll be quick," he added. "I have to leave by six for a dinner reservation."

"I'll be right there." She texted Charlie:

> Rosie: The boss wants to meet now, but I'll be done by 6. Can you wait for me?

> Charlie: Yikes! I hope he has good news. We'll meet you at the bar.

Now, Rosie would need to wait even longer to find out why Drew was joining them. Though she was desperate to know more, she couldn't afford to lose focus. She silenced her phone and stashed it in the pocket of her blazer.

Seeing that Preston's office door was open, she poked her head in. "May I come in?"

"Of course. I was just finishing up with your file. Give me a second."

She eased into the rolling chair across from his desk, hoping he wouldn't keep her for too long. Like her last boss, he was a wealthy white dude in his thirties whose wardrobe was "all Brooks Brothers, all the time." Ever since his arrival last month as the new general manager, or GM, of the Duchess, she'd only had a handful of personal interactions with him. Most of the time, he communicated via phone or email.

He turned his attention away from his computer. "Rosalina?"

"Just Rosie, please."

"All right, Rosie. I'm impressed with your file. In the seven years you've been at the Duchess, you've done well for yourself. When you started out, you were a lowly front desk clerk, and now you're the assistant general manager. That's quite an achievement."

Lowly? Not cool, bro. Despite her discomfort, she kept her bright smile in place. "Thank you, sir. I realize it was a quick trajectory, but I'm really dedicated, and I love it here."

Saying it made her sound like a kiss-ass, but it was the truth. She'd always put her whole heart into her job, even back when she'd first been hired at age twenty-two. As one of the few Latina hoteliers to have risen this high in Victoria's competitive hospitality market, she'd worked extra hard to get ahead.

Her boss's gaze flickered back to his computer screen. "While your past accomplishments were admirable, that's not what I called you here to discuss. Right now, I'm more concerned about the future of this hotel. It's no secret that the previous GM did a terrible job. For that reason, the Duchess needs a fresh start. A reboot like the one I carried out when I ran the Devonshire. Have I mentioned my experiences there?"

Only three or four times. "Yes, and your stories were very inspiring."

"So I've been told. Not everyone could do what I did—take an outdated hotel and turn it into a well-reviewed gem—but I achieved it in less than a year."

While Rosie had no desire to hear more Devonshire stories, she leaned forward, as if riveted by his words.

He continued. "I started by getting rid of the deadwood, and that's what I intend to do here. For far too long, the Duchess has languished in the shadow of the Grand Duke. My goal is to reclaim some of our former glory, but I can't do it unless my team is fully on board. And I'm not sure if that's the case."

Rosie's pulse sped up. Ever since he'd taken the reins, she and the other senior staff had been on edge. They were afraid he'd replace all of them with his own people, which wasn't an unusual move in the hotel business.

But even if he recruited the most highly trained managers in all of Canada, the Duchess would *never* be at the same level as its hated rival, the world-famous Grand Duke Hotel. Designed to resemble a massive French chateau, the Duke boasted over four hundred rooms, two grand ballrooms, and a well-reviewed restaurant. It stretched over an entire city block, occupying prime real estate across from Victoria's popular Inner Harbour.

In comparison, the Duchess seemed like an outdated relic from a bygone era. Though it had flourished in the 1920s and '30s as an iconic boutique hotel with an Art Deco vibe, by now, it had lost most of its glamor.

Preston tapped his pen on the table. "Are you aware of our rating on Tripadvisor?"

Rosie flinched. "Last time I checked, it was not quite at four stars. Three point eight, I believe. It was ranked seven point five out of ten on Expedia."

"Mediocre, at best. And our occupancy rate hasn't risen above seventy percent all year. Meanwhile, the Duke consistently sells out."

"That's true, but they gave all their rooms a total makeover four years ago."

He frowned. "It's hardly an ideal situation. Like I said,

normally I'd clean house, but that seems unnecessarily cruel with the holidays almost upon us."

Rosie smoothed her damp palms over the wool fabric of her skirt. "Thank you, sir."

"You're not off the hook yet. If you'd like to play a key role in my plans to revive the Duchess, then you and your staff need to get this hotel back on track. I want you to lean into the holidays —*hard*. Make us a must-stay destination for couples and families traveling in December. Push our occupancy rate to at least ninety percent."

He couldn't be serious. Given that it was the first week of November, she'd need a Christmas miracle to make that happen.

She kept her tone upbeat, hoping to hide the fact that she was freaking out internally. "Any thoughts on what you'd like to see? Would you like us to host a few holiday events or offer more amenities?"

"Whatever it takes. Brainstorm with your staff to make the Duchess the most festive, holiday-forward hotel in Victoria. Within reason, since there's not much room in the budget. You'll have to put in a lot of nights and weekends, but if you can turn things around by New Year's, then you and your team can stay."

Longer hours. More stress. And a tight deadline. Not ideal, but better than looking for a new job in January. "I'll do my best, sir."

"Thank you for understanding, Rosie. Considering your excellent track record, it would be a shame to let you go. Have a nice weekend."

It would be a shame to let you go. Not quite a threat, but definitely a warning.

Upon leaving his office, she checked her phone. Though she'd missed a few messages from the Damsels, she didn't have the heart to text them with an update. As much as she hated the thought of losing her job, she was even more concerned about them. What kind of a crappy New Year would it be if they ended up unemployed? For their sake, she'd do everything she could to meet Preston's expectations.

Before heading to the hotel bar, she dashed into the washroom to freshen up. Under the bright bulbs, her light brown skin appeared paler than usual, making the bags under her eyes stand out. She freed her hair from its confining bun, letting the dark, wavy strands fall to her shoulders, then gave her lipstick and mascara a quick touch-up.

Normally, she wouldn't fuss over her appearance, but with Drew coming to happy hour, she didn't want to look like a complete wreck.

Stop worrying about him.

If anything, she should be glad for the chance to see him again.

But right now, she had a *lot* on her plate.

Not only was she expected to perform miracles at work, but once the holidays ramped up, the onslaught of family get-togethers would begin. The Gonzalez clan loved any excuse to celebrate. Which wasn't a bad thing, except for the part where she'd be under more scrutiny than usual since she was still single at the ripe old age of twenty-nine. Worse yet, she'd have to endure more of her family's awkward matchmaking attempts.

Best not to think about that now.

She walked through the lobby, which was painfully empty for a Friday night. Though the plush gray couches offered an inviting place to sit, they were unoccupied, as were the matching armchairs clustered around the tiled fireplace along the south wall. At the front desk, two clerks stood on duty, looking bored. She greeted them, then made her way to the Gilded Lily, the hotel's cocktail lounge.

The 1920s-style bar was one of the hotel's best features, decorated with green glass pendant lights, a tin-tiled ceiling, and brown leather club chairs. One wall displayed framed newspaper articles and photos from the twenties, along with vintage Art Deco posters. Unlike the lobby, it was half-full, mostly men and women in business suits who were probably attending the nearby convention on risk management.

Two of the Damsels—Charlie and Selena—were perched on leather stools beside the bar top, chatting with Knox, the head bartender. The two women made quite the contrast. Charlie was a petite, bubbly white woman with wide green eyes and an ash-blond pixie cut, whereas Selena was tall and shapely, with sleek black hair and a sharp wit. Like Rosie, she was of Mexican descent, fluent in Spanish, and had gotten her start at the Duchess by working as a front desk clerk. She now played an integral role as the hotel's food and beverage manager.

Charlie's brow furrowed as she greeted Rosie. "Are you okay? How was your review? Was it bad? You have those little stress lines on your forehead."

"Is Preston going to fire you?" Selena asked. "Is he going to fire *all* of us? Please, no. I have to pay off my credit card debt."

"No one's getting fired," Rosie said. "Not yet."

Knox nodded her way. "Need a drink, Rosie? Shot of tequila? You look like you could use one." He always spoke with a growl in his voice. The gruff, bearded bartender wasn't known for being warm and fuzzy, but his mixology skills were unsurpassed. And it was no secret—at least not to Rosie—that Charlie had spent the past year pining for him.

"Thanks, but I'll wait until we get to Pepe's," Rosie said. "I've already spent enough time at the Duchess this week."

"Fine," Knox grumbled. "First, tell me if I've still got a job."

"Everyone's okay for now, but the next two months might be kinda stressful." She wished she could offer more reassurance, but she didn't want to lie. She glanced around the bar, looking for the fourth member of the Damsels. "Is Laurel coming? It's not like her to miss out."

"She went home early to get ready for her cousin's wedding." Selena slid off her stool. "Let's go. I told Drew we'd be there around five thirty, and it's almost six."

"Hang on," Rosie said. "When did you decide to invite him to happy hour?"

"It was a last-minute thing," Selena said. "This morning, I had a training session with him at Northlife. My regular trainer had to cancel, so he filled in for her. I told him we were going out tonight and suggested he join us. It's no big deal."

Maybe not to Selena. But to Rosie, seeing Drew again was a *very* big deal.

Last year, in her role as assistant manager, she'd negotiated an agreement with Northlife Fitness, the mega-gym located just around the corner from the hotel. Since the Duchess didn't have an in-house workout room, the hotel's guests received courtesy passes to the gym. As part of the deal, she'd also wrangled a discounted membership rate for the hotel staff.

Eager to take advantage, she'd signed up for ten weight lifting sessions with Drew Richardson, the club's most popular personal trainer. Despite wanting to respect their boundaries as client and trainer, her attraction to him had grown into a full-blown crush.

She still wished she'd been open with him about her feelings.

Maybe if she had, he wouldn't have gone after Evelyn, the stunning blond woman who taught the advanced spin classes. Once they'd started dating, Rosie had let her gym membership lapse rather than risk running into them. Not exactly a mature decision, but at the time, she'd also been dealing with an increased workload and a hefty dose of family drama.

Following Selena and Charlie, she left the Gilded Lily, then walked with them out of the hotel's entrance. Outside, the air was brisk, and a light drizzle was falling. She shivered, pulling her wool peacoat tighter around herself.

Charlie placed a hand on her arm. "Are you upset Drew's joining us?"

"Not upset. Just surprised," Rosie said. "I wish I'd had a little more warning."

"And given you a chance to bail?" Selena said. "No way."

"I wouldn't have bailed," Rosie muttered. "Happy hour means too much to me. Besides, it doesn't matter if Drew's there or not. He's taken."

Charlie grinned. "Not anymore. Selena told me he's totally single."

"He is?" Rosie demanded, then cringed at how desperate she sounded.

Selena smirked. "Yep. He and Evelyn broke up in August. Something you would have known if you ever came crawling back to the gym."

Rosie groaned. "I wanted to, but it was too hard seeing them together constantly."

"Fair enough," Selena said. "And for the record, I wouldn't have asked him to join us if he was still with his ex. But when I talked to him, he seemed excited to grab a drink. I think he's been having a hard time. I'm not sure if it's related to his breakup or something else."

For months, Rosie had wished he was still a part of her life. Even if her romantic feelings for him had been one-sided, she'd always enjoyed chatting with him during their workouts. Maybe now, she could rekindle their friendship.

"I'm glad he's coming," she said. "It'll be nice to see him again."

It was just one drink. What was the worst that could happen?

Two

DREW RICHARDSON WONDERED IF HE'D BEEN STOOD UP. Selena had told him they'd be meeting at Pepe's Cantina around five thirty, and it was six now. The place was packed, but he'd snagged the last available high-top. A Latin pop song came on, and he bopped his head to the music, trying to stay upbeat. The Damsels were probably just running late.

When his phone buzzed, he pulled it out of his pocket.

Selena: Sorry to make you wait. Just leaving the hotel now.

Drew: Great! Grabbed us a table near the bar.

Knowing he wouldn't be drinking alone, he signaled his server over and ordered a pitcher of the house margaritas, along with chips and salsa. Was it a little pathetic that he'd spent all day looking forward to tonight's happy hour? Maybe so, but he'd been mired in a broody funk for the past two days. Having Selena show up on his training schedule had been a stroke of luck. When she'd extended tonight's invitation, he'd accepted right away.

More than anything, he was eager to see Rosie again. He'd

really missed her friendship. Back in February, after months of working out at Northlife three or four times a week and training with him on Thursdays, she'd just stopped coming. When he'd texted her to see if everything was okay, she'd claimed her life was too busy to squeeze in time for the gym. Though he knew how demanding her job was, he couldn't help worrying that he'd driven her away.

Back when he'd first met her, a little over a year ago, he'd felt a powerful—and unexpected—wave of attraction every time they worked out together. Normally, he never hit on the women he trained. Above all, he wanted them to feel safe around him. But Rosie's outgoing nature, combined with her candid sense of humor and enticing curves, had lit a fire in him. So much that he'd considered asking one of his coworkers to take over as her personal trainer, just so he'd be free to date her.

But before he made his move, Evelyn had walked into his life. Up until then, he'd kept his relationships casual. A lot of hookups. A few girlfriends, but none who'd ever captured his heart. Having spent years watching his parents' marriage slowly disintegrate, he didn't have much faith in romantic relationships. Until Evelyn had woven her spell over him. Little by little, she'd gained his trust, only to dump him for Jared, who just happened to be his direct supervisor.

It had been rough.

Drew didn't want her back, but since they worked together, avoiding her was impossible. And two days ago, she'd invited him to her December wedding. Truly, the icing on the shit cake.

Ever since then, he'd been stewing over it, but he was tired of wallowing. He desperately wanted to get his groove back so that he could enjoy the holiday season. Maybe tonight could be the first step.

Selena breezed into Pepe's with Charlie and Rosie trailing in her wake. She waved at Drew. "Hey there. Thanks for grabbing a table. This place is hopping."

He grinned at them, unable to hide his glee at the sight of Rosie. She looked paler than he remembered but still as alluring as ever. Thick, black hair falling in waves to her shoulders, big dark eyes with crazy-long lashes, and full, kissable lips. Even clad in business attire, she was sexy as hell, wearing a pencil skirt that accentuated her shapely butt.

"Hey, Damsels," he said. "Thanks for letting me crash your happy hour. I ordered us a pitcher of margaritas."

"Good call," Charlie said. "I'm dying for a drink. A bunch of conventioneers arrived yesterday, and holy cats, have they been demanding."

"I hear you," Drew said. "A few of them came to use the gym this morning, and they were pissed because we don't have a lap pool."

Rosie flashed him a shy smile. "Hi, Drew."

"Hey, Rosie. Good to see you again." He wasn't going to ask why she hadn't been back to the gym in months. All that mattered was that she'd shown up tonight.

Their server arrived and set down the pitcher and glasses, along with two baskets of tortilla chips and three bowls of Pepe's famous salsa: Medium, Hot, and "Disco Inferno." After pouring margaritas for all of them, Drew raised his glass. "A toast—to the Damsels."

"Hell, yes," Selena said. "We need it, given that our jobs are on the line."

Drew kept his gaze focused on Rosie, whose smile had suddenly vanished. "Everything okay at the hotel?" he asked.

She sighed. "It's not that bad, but we have a huge challenge ahead of us."

"Don't keep us in suspense any longer," Charlie said. "Spill."

Sensing Rosie's hesitancy, Drew spoke up quickly. "I won't reveal a word, I promise. What happens at happy hour stays at happy hour."

"Let me get some booze into my system first." Rosie took a

long drink of her margarita before describing her meeting with the hotel's new general manager. Her voice was grave as she outlined his expectations.

Drew wished he could help. Like everyone who worked with the Duchess, he knew the place sorely needed renovations. He also knew the last manager had done a shitty job. But Rosie and her team worked their asses off. It wasn't fair that the new guy could threaten to fire them just because he wanted a fresh start. Though he'd given them a chance to save their jobs, attracting more guests during the holiday season sounded like a ton of work.

"I'm sorry to drop this on you," Rosie said to Selena and Charlie. "It's a big bombshell, and I know it wasn't what you were hoping to hear tonight."

"It's not your fault," Charlie said. "Ever since we got a new GM, I was worried something like this might happen."

"Same here," Selena added. "At least we know you're willing to fight for us."

"I'm willing to do whatever it takes to keep you both at the Duchess." Rosie's voice wobbled. "Not just you, but all the staff. I don't want to lose anyone."

Drew regarded her with admiration. Even though she was probably the most at risk of losing her job, she was more concerned about her team than herself.

"Just let us know what you need." Selena topped up everyone's glass, then called their server over and ordered another pitcher. "Even if it means working extra hours, I'm in."

"I'm in, too," Charlie said. "Though I think our boss is delusional if he believes we could ever match the popularity of the Grand Duke. That place is an institution."

More than once, Drew had heard stories about the rivalry between the two hotels, but he'd never understood why it went so deep. "This might sound clueless, but why do you consider the Grand Duke your biggest rival? There are lots of other upscale hotels in downtown Victoria. Maybe they aren't as famous as the Duke, but they're definitely your competition. Right?"

Rosie rubbed her forehead, as though the very thought gave her a headache. "You're not clueless. The question comes up all the time with our new hires. It's because of the Lyons family. Back in the 1920s, they built the two hotels to complement each other. That's why they're only a block apart."

"They're like a big brother and a little sister," Charlie added.

"When the Lyons sold the Duke to a major hotel chain, some members of the family resented it," Rosie said. "They refused to sell the Duchess, hoping its status as an historic boutique hotel would still draw in guests. And it did...for a while."

"But when the Duke's new owners spent a fortune updating it, the place soared in popularity," Charlie said. "The Duchess couldn't keep up. From what I understand, the family planned to bring it up to speed ten years ago, but they didn't have the money. Meanwhile, the Duke's star has kept rising. It's currently the top-rated hotel in all of Victoria."

"So, the Lyons family resents the Duke for its success?" Drew asked.

"With a *vengeance*." Rosie pounded the table with her fist. "Other hotels might be our competition, but the Duke is our sworn enemy."

She said it with such emphasis that Drew laughed. Watching her get fired up about her hotel was something he'd always enjoyed. "That's how my gym feels about KanaFlex. They have over two hundred locations in Canada, and they're always cutting their rates to attract new members." Realizing he was derailing the conversation, he shot Rosie an apologetic look. "Sorry. I didn't mean to get you off track."

"It's fine," she said. "But we need to focus on our game plan for the Duchess."

"I think amping up our Christmas spirit could be fun," Charlie said. "I'll make sure the front desk is brimming with holiday cheer. If our decorating budget doesn't cover it, we can bring in stuff from home. We should also give out cookies at check-in, like they do at the Doubletree. The night auditor makes a mean spritz cookie."

"Cookies are great and all," Selena said, "but how are travelers going to know the Duchess is 'holiday forward' or whatever?"

"We'll have to get the word out as soon as possible," Rosie said. "Maybe then we can draw in visitors who haven't booked hotels for December yet."

Selena snapped her fingers. "I just thought of another perk we could offer. Remember when we used to host a weekday happy hour for our guests at the cocktail lounge? They loved the free wine and cheese. Our last GM nixed it, but we could start it up again, this time with festive seasonal cocktails."

"Great idea," Rosie said. "Those happy hours were always a big hit."

Drew spoke up, eager to contribute to the conversation. "How about adding some family-friendly activities on the weekends? Like cookie decorating or Christmas crafts? My sister's a preschool teacher, so I could get some ideas from her."

Rosie beamed at him. "I like it. Those activities could get messy, but we could set them up in the breakfast room. One of our main goals is to draw in more families."

Her grateful smile filled him with a warm glow. He kept going, wanting to win her over. "You could also provide a hot cocoa bar in the breakfast room on Friday or Saturday nights. With different toppings, like whipped cream, sprinkles, and crushed-up candy canes."

"Yum. Now I want hot chocolate." Charlie grabbed a handful of tortilla chips from the basket. "What if we combined the cocoa night with a Christmas carol sing-along? Wouldn't that be fun? And if we decide to host weekend activities for families, we should have someone dressed as Santa. The kids could visit him, like they do at the mall."

Rosie frowned. "Those Santas are dubious at best. The last time I took my youngest cousin to see Santa at Mayfair Mall, the guy reeked of booze."

Before he could overthink his decision, Drew spoke up. "I'll do it. I've got a Santa suit."

Selena arched her eyebrows at him. "Do you, now? Is this a kink of yours?"

Charlie smacked her in the arm. "What the heck, Selena?"

Selena shrugged. "I'm just saying. There's something about a sexy Santa that makes a lot of women swoon. Last year, I read a bunch of steamy romances with that exact premise. Some of them made me wish a hot Santa would come down *my* chimney."

Heat rose in Drew's cheeks, but he hoped the restaurant's lighting was too dim for the women to notice. It wasn't that he was flustered by Selena's off-color comments; he just didn't want Rosie to think he was using the Santa suit to act out his secret desires.

Then again…given the way she was staring at him, her lips slightly parted, her eyes wide, he wondered if any of her romantic fantasies involved a sexy Santa.

He pushed the thought aside before his brain flooded with racy images. "For your information, I have the suit because I visit shelters and hospitals as a volunteer Santa."

It had started as a dare among his fellow trainers at the gym, where the loser of their 5K run had to dress up as Santa for their holiday party. Rather than whine about coming in last, Drew had fully embraced the part. He'd enjoyed it so much that he'd bought his own suit and put out the word he was available to volunteer. Over the past two years, the Santa gig had brought him a lot of joy. It had also helped make up for a shit-ton of rotten Christmas memories. Something about the holidays had always brought out the worst in his parents.

The grin Rosie gave him was all the validation he needed. "Convinced yet?" he asked her. If nothing else, playing Santa would give him a chance to get close to her again.

"You're hired," she said. "Or, rather, you're volunteered because I can't afford to pay you."

"It's okay. Consider it my good deed for the holidays." He was so focused on Rosie and the adorable way she was beaming at him that he almost missed Selena leaning down to whisper in Charlie's ear. Both women stood up hastily and placed a couple of twenties on the table.

"This will cover our share," Selena said. "We have to take off. We've got...that thing."

"What thing?" Rosie asked. "What am I missing?"

"Nothing major," Charlie said. "I'm going over to Selena's to help her with...um..."

Selena grabbed her purse. "With my Instant Pot. I got one on sale and can't figure it out."

"But you don't cook," Rosie said.

"Exactly!" Charlie replied. "That's why I'm helping her. See you later!"

Drew watched them go, confused by the whole exchange. It wasn't like Rosie's friends to leave her in the lurch. He turned to face her. "What's up with those two?"

She rolled her eyes. "I think we've been set up."

Three

THE NEXT TIME ROSIE SAW SELENA AND CHARLIE, SHE was having words with them. *Stern* words. Where did they get off, engineering such a blatant setup?

She glanced across the table at Drew, who seemed befuddled by their hasty exit.

Why did he have to look so good? And was she shallow as hell for still drooling over him?

To be fair, he was objectively hot. He worked as a personal trainer, and when he wasn't at the gym, he spent his free time pursuing outdoor activities like kayaking, hiking, and biking, which meant his body was in amazing shape. Six feet tall, lean and muscular, with short brown hair, warm chocolate-brown eyes, and dimples for days. Plus, he was so thoughtful. It was no surprise the "Golden Oldies" clique at the gym—a group of women in their seventies and eighties—treated him like their honorary grandson.

Who could resist a guy like that?

But even if Rosie had been enjoying his company tonight, she didn't like the way their happy hour had turned into an impromptu date. She looked down at her glass, which was almost empty. By now, she'd had the equivalent of two and a half margaritas. Maybe she should call it a night. She was about to excuse herself when Drew cleared his throat.

She forced herself to look up at him, which was a mistake because those soulful brown eyes sucked her right in. "Yes?"

"Can I ask you something?" His voice carried an unexpected vulnerability.

With a twinge of guilt, she remembered what Selena had told her. Something about Drew having a hard time. But they'd gotten so caught up in discussing their plans for the Duchess that none of them had asked him how he was doing.

"Sure," she said. "Is everything okay?"

"Sort of. But since we're alone, I need to know—did I do something to offend you last winter?"

Where had that come from? "What? *No.* Why would you think that?"

"You haven't been back to the gym since February. You said you were busy, but I wondered if I screwed up somehow." He ran a finger around the rim of his glass. "I try to treat all my clients with respect, but if I offended you or behaved inappropriately, I'd like to know what I did. Was it my fault?"

It was, but not for the reasons he thought. After months of secretly yearning for him, her self-worth had dwindled when he began dating Evelyn. No matter how much Rosie worked out, she'd *never* look that good. Despite her firm belief in embracing body positivity, she hadn't been able to shake the nagging insecurity that cropped up whenever she compared herself to his girlfriend.

She couldn't tell him that, but she could be honest about the other factors that had led to her decision. "It wasn't you. Life just got really busy. My last boss was so incompetent that we had a mass exodus of staff, and I ended up taking on more responsibility at the hotel. Then my dad had a heart attack in April, so I tried to visit him whenever I could."

"Oh, shit, Rosie. I'm sorry."

"It's okay." She wiped her eyes quickly, remembering how agonizing those months had been. "The doctor said it was a warning. My dad needs to exercise more and watch his diet. But he wasn't happy about it, and the stress was hell on my mom. I should have told you what was going on, though you probably would have reminded me that being physically active is a great way to relieve tension."

"Maybe so, but I wouldn't have pressured you. You don't have to come back to the gym if you don't want to."

"I've been walking a lot, but..." It wasn't the same. Even if she'd never considered herself a gym person, she'd genuinely enjoyed those early morning workouts. She and Selena had gotten into the habit of going before work, then grabbing smoothies for breakfast. Their routine had energized her. "After the holidays, I'll think about re-upping my membership. Right now, I have too much going on."

When her phone pinged with the distinctive chime she'd given her mom, she pulled it out. "Can you hang on a sec? My mom sent me a message, and I've learned to ignore her at my own peril." When he nodded, she took a peek.

Mamá: You're coming for Sunday dinner.
Right??

Of course she was. Twice a month, her parents hosted a big family dinner at their place. The few times she'd skipped out due to the demands of her job, she'd gotten a blistering lecture on priorities from her mom.

Rosie: I'll be there at six. Do you need me to bring anything?

Mamá: Just your biggest smile. Jaime invited one of his coworkers to join us for dinner. He's eager to meet you!!

"Fuck me," she muttered. Realizing she'd said it out loud, a warm flush heated her cheeks. "Sorry, but my mom reminded me I'm expected for dinner this Sunday."

"Is that good or bad?"

"Mostly good. I like spending time with my family, but they're always up in my business. And..." She hesitated, then decided to be honest. "Whenever they criticize my life choices, I end up feeling pathetic."

"What can they possibly have to criticize? You're the assistant manager of the Duchess. That's so impressive."

"Thanks, but it doesn't make up for the fact that I'm still single. My parents think it's because I work too hard. They're afraid I'm so obsessed with my career that I'll never settle down." She sighed, remembering how Mamá had nagged her at the last dinner, tossing in the painful phrase, "We just want you to be happy."

Rosie would be a lot happier if her parents would back off a little. While she sometimes envied her older brother and younger sister—both of whom were happily married—she was so focused on her job that her dating life came second. Not to mention, the last time she'd made an effort, she'd ended up with a boyfriend who'd torpedoed her self-esteem.

"Are your folks really traditional?" he asked. "I don't want to assume they are, but..."

"But it's okay to ask. My grandparents on both sides were originally from Mexico, so they placed a lot of emphasis on the importance of family. And religion. But my parents are more laid-back since they grew up here in Victoria. Even so, they'd love to have as many grandkids as possible."

"That's a tall order. Have they been trying to set you up with anyone?"

"Yep, and it's only going to get worse because my whole family goes hard at the holidays. And thanks to my boss, my stress levels are already off the charts." She tossed back the rest of her margarita. "Sorry. Didn't mean to off-load all my baggage onto you."

"I don't mind." He gestured toward her glass. "Want another drink?"

"I'd better not. I've barely eaten anything all day." But she was reluctant to leave. This was the longest conversation she'd had with Drew in months. She'd forgotten how much she enjoyed talking to him during her training sessions. Mostly, they'd kept things light—chatting about their favorite movies or their weekend plans—but she'd always looked forward to it.

"Why don't we order some food?" he said. "Then you won't be drinking on an empty stomach."

She didn't want to read too much into his suggestion, but it seemed like he *wanted* her to stay. "Okay. I can never say no to Pepe's carne asada tacos."

After they put in their order, he focused on her again, giving her a roguish grin that made her pulse race. "Seeing as how I'm swooping in to save the Duchess with my masterful Santa impersonation, is there any way I could help with your family? What if Santa just happened to show up at those Sunday dinners?"

"I *love* that idea. But honestly? I'd rather have Santa bring me an imaginary boyfriend. If my mom believed I was involved with someone, she'd give me a little breathing room. As would the rest of my family." Fully aware of how ludicrous she sounded, she started laughing. "That came out totally unhinged. I blame the tequila."

"I get it. Maybe Santa could bring me a plus-one so that I don't have to attend my ex's wedding without a date. I'm dreading it like the plague."

Which ex was he talking about? "Do you mean Evelyn? Didn't you two *just* break up?"

"Pretty much. She left me three months ago for another trainer. Not just any trainer, but my supervisor, Jared."

What a shitty move. "Ouch. That sucks."

"Yeah, it was brutal." He released a ragged breath. "The worst part was—I kind of saw it coming. Back in May, when he was hired at Northlife, I was worried because he and Evelyn had a history together. Two years ago, they worked at the same gym in Vancouver and dated on and off. But when I brought it up to Evelyn, she said I was being paranoid."

Rosie's jaw tightened. *Classic gaslighting.* She'd been through it before.

He continued. "In August, Evelyn admitted they'd been sneaking around behind my back. Then she chose him over me, which was a tough blow. But not as bad as getting their wedding invitation two days ago. They're getting married on December twenty-second."

Holy shit. Rosie's heart went out to Drew. "I'm sorry. Do...do you still have feelings for her?"

"Not anymore." He looked down and wiped up a stray drop of salsa with his napkin. "Toward the end, things got ugly. We were arguing constantly. It was a relief when she finally told me the truth. But because we work at the same gym, the rest of the staff are concerned about me. Especially after she invited *all* of us to her wedding."

Rosie could only imagine how painful that would be. "You're not going, are you?"

"I'd like to." He met her eyes again. "Maybe it's childish, but I want to prove to her—and everyone else—that I'm doing just fine."

She wanted to reach over and take his hand—anything to console him—but wasn't sure she should cross that line. Instead, she tried to lighten the mood. "That sounds excruciating, though not as grueling as multiple family events where I'm forced to make small talk with a complete stranger."

"I'll trade you," he said. "Or wait..."

"What? Do you want to make a bet? To see whose holiday

season is going to be worse?" She snatched up the last few tortilla chips from the basket.

"Nope. But I do have an idea that might spare us a little agony."

BEFORE DREW COULD SHARE HIS IDEA, THE SERVER arrived with their tacos and a fresh round of drinks. Since they'd have to drive home eventually, they'd both ordered Jarritos soda rather than more margaritas. He pushed aside the empty basket of tortilla chips to make room for their plates.

Upon taking the first bite of her taco, Rosie let out a groan of pleasure. "Mmmm. I was so hungry. Today's sad desk lunch was an apple and a bag of pretzels from the vending machine."

Even if that groan hadn't been directed at him, Drew's groin tightened. Fuck, she was sexy. He'd really missed her. Missed her laugh, her self-deprecating humor, and her quirky passion for action movies. She'd seen tons of them, even the janky, low-budget ones that went direct to streaming. They'd once spent an entire workout ranking the movies in the *Fast & Furious* franchise.

But then he'd gotten involved with Evelyn, who'd put him through the wringer. Once he was single again, he'd thought about reaching out to Rosie but hesitated because he worried that he'd driven her away from the gym. Now that he understood why she'd been absent, he wished he could have supported her when she'd been dealing with her dad's health issues.

Rosie added a spoonful of salsa to her taco. "What's your idea?"

"You need a date for a few dinners and some holiday events, right? Just to get your parents off your back for a while?"

"Yeah. What with everything going on at the hotel, I'm at my limit."

"And I want to get the wedding-from-hell over with. So, here's a thought. Why don't you come as my plus-one? In return, you can bring me home and tell your folks we're dating."

As he waited for her to respond, sweat beaded on his forehead. Was it nerves or a reaction to the "Disco Inferno" salsa he'd added to his taco?

Rosie narrowed her eyes. "Are you punking me? This is a rom-com scenario. No one *actually* fake dates in real life."

"Maybe they don't, but it's a decent plan." He paused, afraid he'd insulted her. He didn't want her to think she wasn't worthy of a real date. "It's not that I'm opposed to actual dating, but I'm not in a good place for a romantic relationship. Not after all the shit I went through with Evelyn. And..."

He stopped before he unloaded any further. His issues stemmed from his teenage years, when his parents had turned their house into a battlefield, but he wasn't about to burden her with all that baggage.

"I don't have any room in my life for romantic entanglements, either," Rosie said. "Not with my job hanging by a thread. And I *definitely* don't have the bandwidth to massage some guy's ego when he yells at me for not spending enough time with him."

The bitterness in her voice made Drew suspect she was speaking from experience. "I take it that's happened before?"

"Yep. Not a great scene." She finished her taco in a couple of bites.

When she didn't elaborate, he knew better than to probe any further. Like him, she'd probably experienced her share of heartache. All the more reason his fake-dating scenario was a solid plan. "So...would you be on board with this idea?"

She laughed. "As wild as it sounds, I might be up for it, except for the part where I'd be lying to my family."

Yet another reason why he admired her. Even if her family irritated her, she didn't want to hurt them. "I don't like lying, either, but given how much time we'd be spending together, it would almost be like we're dating for real. Except without all the angst and expectations."

"If we do this, you wouldn't just be coming to my parents' house for our Sunday dinners. You'd need to attend my family's big holiday events: my aunt's party on the sixteenth, our Nochebuena celebration on Christmas Eve, and Three Kings Day on January sixth. It might cut into your time with your own family."

He gave a curt laugh. "Fine with me." At her shocked expression, he rushed to explain. "I'm not close to my parents. My sister and I might try to visit them on Christmas Day for a few hours, but that's all we can handle."

"I'm sorry."

"I've learned to live with it." Most of the time, he rarely mentioned his parents or his fractured past. Instead, he locked that shit up tight so it couldn't hurt him anymore. No matter how miserable he'd been, he'd managed to make a good life for himself. "Anyway...you didn't answer me. Rosie Gonzalez, would you be my pretend girlfriend for the next two months?"

Instead of agreeing immediately, she gnawed on her lip, clearly torn over her decision. Which made him suspect he'd grossly overstepped.

What were you thinking? You finally get a chance to reconnect with Rosie, and then you ask her if she wants to pretend you're dating. Who does that?

He was tempted to blame the tequila, but he wasn't even drunk.

"Never mind. It was a goofy idea." He raised his glass in a salute. "Who knows—maybe you'll hit it off with the next guy your family invites to dinner."

"If he's one of my brother's colleagues, then he's a dentist. He could look exactly like Pedro Pascal, and I still wouldn't be interested. Not if he's going to nag me about flossing my teeth, which my brother does on the regular." She gave a full-body shudder. "If we agree to this, then what do we tell people when January seventh rolls around?"

Shit. He'd been so focused on surviving Evelyn's wedding that he hadn't considered what he and Rosie would do after the holidays. "How about we say it didn't work out because our jobs are too demanding? Or make up some other excuse? Would that be okay?"

As he waited for her to respond, he crumpled his napkin into a tiny ball. To his immense relief, her lips quirked up in an affectionate smile.

"All right, I'm in," she said. "This Sunday at six, you're joining me at my parents' house for dinner. Bring your A-game, *sweetheart.*"

Perfect. Whatever nickname she wanted to give him, he'd answer to it.

 Four

52 Days Until Christmas

A blast of wind buffeted Rosie as she and Charlie walked along the paved path overlooking the ocean. Below them, the stiff breeze whipped the waves into whitecaps. Rosie inhaled the briny scent and wiped the spray from her face. Fishing her knitted gloves from the pocket of her fleece jacket, she put them on and tugged her woolen toque tighter onto her head.

"I can't believe you wanted to go walking today," Charlie said. "I was sure you were going to suggest we go for coffee instead."

"We can go after. My treat. But I was really wound up last night, and I need to burn off some nervous energy."

An understatement, at best. Rosie had spent most of the night tossing and turning as she considered Drew's proposition. She needed to talk to someone before she took him to dinner at her parents' house, and her Saturday morning ritual with Charlie—a brisk stroll along the Dallas Road walkway—was the ideal setting. In the summer and fall months, the oceanfront path was usually crowded with dog walkers, joggers, and families, but today, it was practically empty.

"Are you worried about the next two months at the Duchess?"

Charlie asked. "Don't be. We're going to crush it. Preston's gonna be so impressed."

"Thanks, but that wasn't what kept me awake."

"Was it Drew?" Charlie's voice rose an octave. "Did something happen after we left? I knew I sensed a romantic vibe between the two of you."

"Is that why you and Selena made up that half-assed excuse? There's no way she'd buy an Instant Pot. She hates all forms of cooking."

"I'll admit it was weak, but I was trying to improvise. You and Drew were bonding, and we wanted to give you some space. Was it the sexy Santa thing that did it for you? Drew would make a seriously hot Santa."

Rosie sighed. When she'd gone to bed last night, the idea of Drew playing Santa had spurred a delicious set of fantasies. Like the one where she was sitting naked on his lap and asking him what she could do to get on the "nice list." But her naughty dreams weren't the cause of her restless slumber. She still couldn't believe she'd accepted his offer.

Honestly, given everything she was dealing with right now—trying to save her job, protect her team, and keep the hotel afloat—she should have turned him down. Drew had even given her the opportunity when he'd called it a goofy idea. But she hadn't been able to resist the thought of spending more time with him.

Hoping for Charlie's support, she told her friend all about it, explaining the no-strings, fake-dating ruse she'd agreed to. Once she finished her confession, she stopped and leaned on the railing overlooking the water. Another blast of spray hit her cheeks, and she wiped it off with her scarf. In the cold light of day, pretending to date someone sounded like the plot of a Hallmark movie.

"It's messed up, isn't it?" she asked. "Should I call Drew and tell him it's off?"

"No!" Charlie turned to face her. "You're totally into him, and he clearly likes spending time with you. Plus, this deal works in your favor. All you have to do is attend one measly wedding, and in return, he'll be spending a ton of time with your family. Aren't your parents' dinners, like, every Sunday?"

"Every other Sunday. But, yeah, they're a lot." Rosie paused. "Does this mean you think it would work?"

"In theory, it sounds solid. But what if you end up wanting more from Drew?"

That exact question had taken root in Rosie's psyche sometime after midnight and had refused to leave. "I don't think that's going to happen. With my job on the line, I've got too much at stake to invest any emotional energy into a real romantic relationship. This way, I won't have to apologize if I'm constantly busy."

Charlie wrapped her scarf tighter around her neck. "I dunno. Even if you're super busy, Drew seems like the kind of guy who could deal with it. Like, his ego wouldn't take a beating because you're not available twenty-four seven."

Rosie wasn't so sure. Her last boyfriend, Erik, had initially praised her for the way she'd risen in the ranks of the Duchess. Until he'd realized she was making more money than him, in a job that was far more demanding. When he left her, he'd claimed it was her fault because she was too obsessed with work to satisfy his needs.

"It's not just about my work schedule," she said. "Drew flat-out told me he didn't want a relationship. His ex really messed with his head. Plus, he's dealing with other baggage."

Charlie resumed walking. "Really? What kind of baggage?"

"He doesn't get along with his parents—so much that he avoids spending time with them at Christmas." His revelation had come as a surprise to Rosie because he'd always seemed so happy-go-lucky. "It actually works in my favor since he's not on the hook for any big holiday events with them. All he needs from me is a date for his ex's wedding. It's a total win-win."

"Are you trying to convince me or yourself?"

"Um...both of us, I guess," Rosie said. "I want this to work. And who knows? Maybe down the road..."

Nope. She wasn't going there. This was a friends-only agreement. Developing feelings of passion—or even love—could lead to serious heartbreak. She couldn't handle the emotional fallout, not when she was already anxious about potentially losing her job in January.

When they approached the long, concrete breakwater that led to the Ogden Point lighthouse, Rosie paused. This part of the path was more exposed to the elements, which meant the spray from the ocean would be even fiercer. Above them, the raucous cries of Victoria's ever-present seagulls rose in volume.

Charlie stopped beside her. "Don't get me wrong—I understand the appeal of a pretend boyfriend. Even if it's just for show, having a plus-one for the holidays sounds like a good deal."

Rosie nudged her. "If you want a date, why don't you ask Knox out?"

"What? *No.* We're just friends. He doesn't think of me that way."

"You sure? Because he's nicer to you than anyone else, which is saying a lot. He's the grumpiest bartender I've ever met. And I know how you feel about him."

"It doesn't matter how I feel. He'd never go for it. Heck, he doesn't even like the holidays." Charlie narrowed her eyes. "Besides, my dating life isn't the issue here."

"Right. Sorry." For now, Rosie would let it go. "So, do you think Drew and I can pull this off?"

"Sure. If you're both on the same page, then it should work. And Drew's a nice guy, so no matter what happens, you'll have fun with him."

"Exactly." Rosie felt a surge of excitement. Not only was this plan going to succeed, but it also might make the next two months more enjoyable. She leaned over and gave her friend a side-hug. "Thanks for the vote of confidence."

"Happy to help." Charlie took off her mittens and blew on her hands, then rubbed them together. "Now, can we go get coffee? This weather is for the birds."

Saturday mornings at Northlife Fitness were chaotic at best. Everyone who was too busy to exercise during the week felt the need to make up for it, plus the schedule was packed with classes from 5:30 a.m. until noon: boot camp, spin, yoga, power lifting, and speed training. The cold, blustery weather had also driven a lot of people indoors.

Having just finished teaching a boot camp class, Drew parked himself at the smoothie bar to fuel up before his next training session. As he sipped his almond butter and banana smoothie, he scrolled through his phone, rereading the messages Rosie had sent him late last night, occasionally chuckling at her snarky tone. To prepare him for Sunday, she'd given him lots of information about her family.

Evelyn snagged the stool next to his. "Drew. How are you doing?"

His jaw tightened at the sight of her. As always, she looked cool and controlled, her blond hair pulled back in a tight ponytail. Though she'd just come from teaching an hourlong spin class, she hadn't broken a sweat.

"I'm okay," he said. "Just catching a break before my next client."

She placed a hand on his knee and lowered her voice. "No, really. How *are* you? I heard you were upset when you got our wedding invitation. I didn't do it out of spite. I literally invited everyone who works here."

Even so, he would have preferred to miss it. "I guess it just seemed so sudden."

"Not really. I've known Jared for over two years. And

honestly? The last time I ended things with him, I kept wondering if I'd made a huge mistake."

"Funny how you never mentioned that to me before," Drew muttered.

"I was trying to move on. But once I reconnected with him, it was obvious he was always the right one for me. I just couldn't see it before."

Never mind that I got caught in the middle.

"I didn't mean to hurt you," she added. "But when you know, you know. Right? You have to follow your heart."

Rather than let her words eat away at him, he struck back. "True. That's why I'm glad I found someone who accepts me for who I am."

She pulled her hand away quickly, but not before an irritated look crossed her face. Knowing he'd blindsided her, he savored the moment. There were times when a little pettiness was incredibly satisfying.

"I didn't realize you'd started dating again." She turned away from him and signaled to the woman behind the counter. "I'll have my usual. A green smoothie with avocado, apple, and extra protein powder."

Drew drank up his smoothie, feeling better with every sip. "I figured it was time to get back out there. Wasn't that what you told me to do after you left?"

She responded with a tight smile. "It's better than wallowing in self-pity. Is she anyone I know?"

"Rosie Gonzalez from the Duchess. I used to be her personal trainer. I think she took a few of your spin classes last year."

"The name doesn't ring a bell, but I'm sure if I saw her, I'd remember. Is it serious?"

Her question put him on the defensive. "Does it matter? You've moved on, so why shouldn't I?"

"Oh, Drew." She released a drawn-out sigh. "This isn't about me. I just hope you're not leading her on. Not when you can't offer her anything."

Not this again. He clenched his hands. "I offered you plenty."

"In bed, sure. But you never gave me your whole heart. That's why I went back to Jared." When he opened his mouth to protest, she held up her hand to stop him. "I tried to make it work with you, but you're emotionally stunted. I'm not sure you're capable of giving more."

She'd told him that before, and he'd tried to change, just for her. After years of casual hookups, he'd been ready to let someone in. To open himself up to a real relationship. But he'd still had a hard time breaking down his walls.

And then she'd gone and destroyed his trust.

"Are you bringing Rosie to the wedding?" she asked.

"Yep. So you can put me down as a 'yes' and include her as my plus-one." The words should have empowered him, but they felt hollow. Even now, three months after Evelyn had ended things, she still had the power to diminish him.

She grabbed her smoothie and stood up. "I'm glad you're coming. But if you're bringing Rosie to get back at me, take her feelings into consideration."

After Evelyn left, he crushed his empty cup and threw it in the trash. She was wrong. He wasn't using Rosie. When he'd proposed this scheme, he'd done it to benefit both of them. They were embarking on it together, with a clear plan and no romantic expectations.

There was no way either of them would end up getting hurt.

Five

For the past year, Rosie had endured countless Sunday dinners where her parents had purposely seated her beside a potential date. Each time, she was forced to make small talk as she fielded the usual questions. Where do you work? Where did you go to university? What do you do for fun? And so on, until the evening felt more like a job interview than a relaxing dinner.

Last month, she'd gotten paired up with Julio—a family friend who was a self-professed film snob. He immediately mocked her love of action movies and told her he preferred foreign films because "they engage me on an intellectual level." *No, thanks.*

The month before that, her dad had invited a guy her age—a friend's son—who'd sounded promising. Until he'd dismissed Rosie's job at the Duchess and denounced hotels as a total rip-off. "I'm more of an Airbnb guy," he'd said. *Hard pass.*

But tonight, with Drew as her date, she wouldn't have to muddle her way through an awkward conversation. Though she'd felt a little guilty about lying to her family, all her remorse vanished when her parents greeted her warmly, thrilled to meet her new "boyfriend." It didn't hurt that Drew had brought them a box of chocolates from Purdy's—a family favorite.

Once dinner was ready, her mom placed her beside Drew at the long wooden table that dominated the family dining room. A table that could be extended by one or two leaves, depending on the size of the gathering. Tonight, only Rosie's immediate family was in attendance—her parents, her siblings and their partners, and her sixteen-month-old niece. All for the best since Drew might have been overwhelmed if the entire Gonzalez clan had shown up.

After Mamá led everyone in saying grace, she turned to Drew. "Since you're our guest of honor, you can go first. I assume you're familiar with Mexican cooking?"

He gave her an affable grin—the kind that could charm any parent. "Mostly tacos, but I'm open to anything."

"Good. The platter nearest to you has chicken enchiladas in salsa verde, and the bowl beside it contains Mexican red rice. The other two bowls have calabacitas— zucchini mixed with tomatoes and corn—and frijoles charros, which are beans with chorizo, bacon, and jalapeño. The melon slices are sprinkled with Tajín, but if you'd prefer plain melon, we have that, too."

He reached for the platter of enchiladas. "Everything looks delicious. I'm glad I brought my appetite."

Mamá beamed at him. "Thank you. It gives me so much pleasure to share a meal with my children on Sunday nights. It's even better when they bring someone special along. Not that my daughter gave me much warning this time."

Rosie's sister, Isabella, took two slices of melon and passed the bowl down the line. "Yeah, Rosie. What's up with that? Last time we talked—which was literally five days ago—Drew's name didn't come up."

"On Thursday, Má asked me to bring one of my colleagues to dinner so he could meet you," Jaime said. "What gives?"

His wife, Camila, glared at him. "Seriously, Jaime? Cut Rosie a little slack. You never even asked her if she was interested."

Rosie was about to respond when Drew rested his hand on her thigh. Though she suspected he was just trying to show his support, his touch sent a tiny shiver along her spine. Feeling bolder, she placed her hand over his. The intimacy of touching him in secret filled her with an unexpected longing.

Don't get carried away. Remember, this isn't real.

She focused on answering her family's questions. "Sorry for not giving you more warning, but Drew and I have actually known each other for a while."

"Really?" Isabella said. "The last time you were dating someone, you wouldn't stop talking about him, and he turned out to be a jerk. So excuse me if I'm a tad dubious about you showing up with a guy you've never mentioned before."

Rosie fought back the urge to snap at her sister. She didn't like being reminded of the mistake she'd made with Erik, trusting him enough to bring him home. His behavior at dinner had been so condescending that she'd spent all evening cringing with guilt.

Drew flashed sad puppy dog eyes at her. "You never mentioned me, honey? Not once? I'm wounded."

Playing along, she gave his shoulder a gentle poke. "Sorry, sweetie. But to be fair, we started as friends."

"Where did you meet?" Isabella demanded.

"At Northlife Fitness—the gym around the corner from the Duchess," Drew said. "I work there as a group fitness instructor and personal trainer. I think it was about a year ago—maybe a little more—when Rosie joined the gym. She took a few of my boot camp classes and then started working with me to concentrate on strength training."

"Ooh, one-on-one personal training." Isabella raised her eyebrows. "I'd like that. It sounds kinda sexy."

"Isabella Maria," Mamá snapped. "Your husband is *right there*." She pointed to Isabella's husband, Peter, who'd ended up with the thankless job of watching over their daughter, Graciela, as she made a mess of her dinner. By the looks of it, more rice had gotten on the tray of her high chair than into her mouth.

Isabella rolled her eyes. "I was just kidding, Má."

"Anyway, after a few months of working out together, Rosie and I grew closer," Drew said. "When she stopped coming to the gym because her life got too hectic, I missed her a lot. But last month, we ran into each other during happy hour, and things just clicked."

Using happy hour as the basis of their story made sense. But rather than admit their meet-up had taken place two days ago, they'd agreed to tell her family it had happened in October.

"That night, Drew asked me out," Rosie said. "We've been together since then. Even though we're both pretty busy, we want to make it work. Don't we, sweetie?" She regarded him with a doting smile. Which was a mistake, because she got so caught up in his deep brown eyes that she could barely pull her gaze away. He was selling it, looking at her like she was the embodiment of his dreams.

"If you've been together for a month, then why is this the first time I'm hearing about it?" Jaime asked. "Why not bring it up at our last dinner?"

"Maybe she didn't want to deal with a ton of questions," Camila said.

Thank you, Camila. Not for the first time, Rosie wondered how her sister-in-law put up with Jaime. "I was about to explain. You all know what a mistake I made with Erik. I hadn't known him for long when I brought him to dinner. Then I regretted it because he didn't fit in."

Mamá clicked her tongue. "That Erik was so wrong for you. I couldn't see the two of you being happy together."

Something she'd harped upon repeatedly. It pained Rosie to admit how right she'd been.

Drew spoke up. "Rosie asked me to keep things quiet until we were sure we wanted to go public. I respected her wishes, even though I desperately wanted to show her off."

"Awww. That's so romantic," Isabella said.

When Drew squeezed Rosie's hand under the table, her arms prickled with goose bumps. Sure it was an act, but he was crushing it.

"Sorry I didn't mention Drew sooner," she said. "I wanted you to meet him because things are going great. In fact, he might be coming to a few of our holiday gatherings."

"*Por supuesto*." Mamá smiled at Drew. "Look how happy you've made my daughter. She's glowing."

While Rosie didn't love being the center of attention, at least she and Drew had successfully convinced her family they were together. If she was lucky, they'd move on to another topic of conversation.

For a few minutes, all was quiet as everyone focused on the food. To Rosie's delight, Drew eagerly accepted a second helping of enchiladas. Mamá always appreciated it when her guests ate heartily. Rosie bumped her thigh against his to get his attention, but when he turned to look at her, his tender expression made her melt inside.

"Everything okay?" he whispered.

She kept her voice low. "Just checking to make sure you're doing all right."

"I'm great. The food is awesome, and your family's so welcoming."

"Hey, you two, no love talk," Isabella said.

"Hush," Mamá said. "Just because you and Peter aren't in your lovey-dovey stage anymore doesn't mean your sister can't enjoy it."

Isabella responded with another of her eye rolls. "It's hard being lovey-dovey when you're looking after a needy toddler and the next baby's due in two months." She turned to Drew and asked sweetly, "So, how do you feel about kids? Do you want any?"

Rosie choked on her rice, then quickly washed it down with a drink of water. She nailed her sister with a flinty glare, but Isabella plastered an innocent smile on her face.

"Eventually, I'd love to have a family, but I've got time," Drew said. "I'm only twenty-seven."

Mamá directed her gaze at him with the intensity of a laser. "You know Rosie's already twenty-nine, right? She doesn't have many fertile years left."

For the love of God.

If Mamá kept this up, she'd scare Drew away. Even though Isabella was pregnant with her second child, and Jamie and Camila were expecting their first one in May, Mamá acted like she wouldn't be truly happy unless all three of her children provided her with grandkids.

Rosie pivoted quickly. "Speaking of kids, Drew's great with them. He teaches a speed training class at the gym for middle school students, and he also volunteered to play Santa at the Duchess. We're starting a new holiday tradition. Every Saturday in December, we're going to offer events geared toward families staying there."

"I was glad to volunteer," Drew said. "It was the least I could do, seeing how Rosie's boss expects her to increase the hotel's occupancy rate during the holidays."

No. Though Drew didn't know better, any hint that Rosie's job was on the line would put her mom on full alert. Like a shark smelling blood in the water, Mamá zeroed in on Rosie. "Why do you need to increase the occupancy rate? Isn't the hotel usually full in December? What with all the holiday events going on in Victoria, there must be a lot of tourists visiting, no?"

"I would think the Duchess would be at full occupancy," Jaime added.

"Like you're an expert on the hospitality industry?" Camila said to him. "You deal with teeth all day."

"I'm not surprised you're having trouble attracting guests," Isabella chimed in. "The last time I looked up the Duchess on

Tripadvisor, it was only ranked number twenty out of all the hotels in Victoria. Even the Days Inn had a higher rating."

Rosie gritted her teeth. "Why were you checking on our ranking?"

Her sister shrugged. "Just curious."

Or because she liked being up in Rosie's business.

"I didn't realize the hotel was struggling that much," her dad said. "Do you think you should look for another job?"

"I wish you'd ended up at the Grand Duke," Mamá added. "It's such a classy hotel." She turned toward Drew. "Did you know Rosie applied there after she finished university? It was her first choice, but they didn't hire her."

"Rosalina always dreamed of working for the Duke," her dad said. "Her great-aunt spent ten years in their housekeeping department and used to tell us stories about it."

Though Rosie had gone through two rounds of interviews at the Duke, she hadn't gotten an offer. At the time, she'd been devastated, but once she'd gotten hired at the Duchess, she'd never considered leaving. For all the ups and downs she'd experienced there, she had no desire to give up her role as assistant manager or lose the support she'd gotten from the Damsels.

"I think the Duchess is lucky to have Rosie," Drew said. "I'm sure she and her team can turn the place around. In fact, last Friday, I helped them brainstorm different holiday activities the hotel could offer their guests. Maybe all of you could give us some more ideas."

Isabella scoffed. "You're talking to the Queen of Christmas. I've got ideas for days. How about a workshop where kids could decorate gingerbread people? I can bake up a bunch for you."

Her enthusiasm took Rosie aback. When was the last time her sister had offered to help her with anything? "That would be fabulous, Iz."

"You know what would be really fun?" Mamá said. "Have the

staff compete in a gingerbread house contest and put them on display. Then the guests can pick their favorite one."

"Yes!" Camila said. "Last year, I watched the Holiday Baking Showdown on the Food Network, and they did a couple of episodes featuring gingerbread houses."

"See if you can get any travel influencers to visit the hotel," Isabella suggested. "I know a few on TikTok if you need some names."

Rosie could hardly believe it. Just like that, her whole family was in her corner. All because Drew had asked their advice—something she hadn't done in years. Usually she wanted them to back off, especially when it came to weighing in on her work life, but she'd never considered soliciting their help.

As Drew continued to encourage them, she felt a twinge of regret. Because even if she didn't need a real boyfriend right now, she wished his support wasn't just an act.

Six

By the time Rosie made it to the hotel's conference room on Tuesday afternoon, Charlie and Selena were already there, along with Laurel—the fourth member of the Damsels—who worked as the hotel's sales and marketing manager. She was a tall white woman with straw-blond hair, freckles, and an easy smile. Though she'd grown up in a rural part of Vancouver Island, she'd come to love living and working in Victoria. She stood at the table, unpacking the food Rosie had ordered for their lunch meeting.

"Sorry I'm late," Rosie said. "I just came from Preston's office. He might stop by the conference room in a bit to hear about our ideas."

Charlie made a face. "I thought this was supposed to be a casual brainstorming session. It won't be casual if he's looking over our shoulders."

"He won't be here for a while yet," Rosie said. "He was about to take a call from the owners about the hotel's numbers."

Hearing that had made her nervous. As a general rule, the owners of the hotel weren't involved in the day-to-day running of the Duchess. But they had to know the hotel's numbers weren't good. A lot of it was due to the ineptitude of the previous GM, an entitled trust fund bro who'd cared more about hosting his buddies than attracting paying guests. Every time Rosie had come to him with an idea for increasing their visibility in Victoria's crowded tourist market, he'd shot her down.

Even if their new boss had high expectations, at least he wanted the Duchess to succeed. While his holiday initiative would entail a lot of work, it could make a difference in the hotel's year-end financials. If the hotel earned enough money, the owners might finally commit to renovating the rooms.

Was that too much to hope for? Maybe so, but Rosie was going to try her hardest. She never did anything halfway.

She went to the front of the conference room, where she'd set up a whiteboard. On it, she wrote down every idea they'd come up with so far, as well as the suggestions her family had offered two nights ago. Today's objective was to winnow them down to a manageable number and figure out how they could put them into action without spending a fortune. After meeting with the hotel's head accountant yesterday, she'd learned their holiday budget was minimal. In the past, it had only been used to cover the expense of decorations in the lobby and the breakfast room.

She pointed to the board. "I put a lot of suggestions up here. Some might not be feasible, but I want us to consider every possible option. Does anyone—"

"Hang on," Selena said. "We're not going to talk about this until we get the scoop on you and Drew. Charlie told me all about your devious dating plan, but she kept it PG. Which doesn't sound nearly as enjoyable as it could be."

Laurel let out a grunt of frustration. "Of course this happened the *one* time I missed out on happy hour. I need more details. My dating life has been so boring that even faking it sounds appealing."

"Faking it?" Selena said. "If there's sex involved, I hope you don't feel the need to fake anything. You deserve as much pleasure as he does."

Rosie rolled her eyes. After her talk with Charlie on Saturday, she'd agreed to let her friend tell the other two Damsels about her agreement with Drew. She just hadn't expected to be grilled on it right away.

"First of all, Drew and I are just friends, so there's nothing R-rated going on. And second, I don't have much to tell. It's only been a few days since we made this arrangement."

"But he went to your parents' house for dinner on Sunday, right?" Charlie said. "How did that go?"

Try as she might, Rosie couldn't stop herself from smiling. "It went great. My mom sent him home with a Rubbermaid container filled with leftovers. He also got my family to brainstorm festive ideas for the hotel."

"What a guy," Laurel said. "Can you explain why you're not dating him for real?"

"Nope." Rosie crossed her arms. "Not when we're on a deadline. We need to focus."

Laurel shot Selena a grin. "You know they're going to end up in bed, don't you?"

"Obviously," Selena said. "And not to objectify Drew, but have you seen him in action on the gym floor? He's got muscles for days."

Rosie resisted the urge to stomp her foot like a toddler. "Can we not discuss this now? Like I said, our new GM might show up, and it wouldn't go over well if he hears us discussing my love life."

That shut them up. Laurel passed out their lunch orders, along with paper plates, cutlery, and napkins. "How should we prioritize all these ideas?" she asked.

"While you're eating, pick your top five choices, then we can discuss them in more detail. Keep in mind that our funds are limited, so we can't do anything too extravagant."

Rosie sat down and grabbed her order—a Montreal smoked meat sandwich on rye, along with a Diet Coke. As she perused the ideas on the board, she tried to stay focused. But despite her best efforts, her thoughts kept drifting to Drew. Last night, they'd talked on the phone for over an hour. Somehow, they'd gone from discussing the Duchess to ranking their favorite holiday movies. Like her, he was a big fan of *Die Hard* and considered it a true Christmas film.

She could get used to this. For the first time in months, she'd gone home from her parents' Sunday dinner feeling good. Not anxious or pathetic. But happy. And not just because she'd brought someone home but also because her family had been so enthusiastic about helping her. Isabella had already scheduled a family baking night so they could whip out an army of gingerbread people.

Rosie tried to clear Drew from her mind. Even if she secretly swooned every time he flashed those dimples, she couldn't get too distracted. Right now, nothing was more important than keeping her job. Not just *her* job but all the Damsels'. If Preston fired them, they'd be facing the prospect of unemployment in the dead of winter. And they'd probably never be lucky enough to work together at the same hotel again.

After finishing her sandwich, she crumpled up the wrapper and tossed it in the bag. "Okay, everyone. Before we share our choices, let's talk about how we're going to promote our holiday activities. Laurel, do you want to hit us with your plan?"

"Definitely. It'll be a lot of work, but my team is excited to dig in." Like Charlie, Laurel tended toward a positive worldview. "Once we decide what we're going to offer, we'll get going right away. Since we can't afford to pay for advertising, we'll have to use whatever free coverage we can get. We'll send out press releases, contact Tourism Victoria and the Chamber of Commerce, update our website, get into local calendars, send out emails, and do a bunch of social media blasts."

"That's great," Rosie said. "My sister knows a few travel influencers who might be willing to visit the hotel."

Laurel's eyes widened. "Really? That kind of exposure could make a difference. Tell your sister I'll be forever in her debt if she can come through."

Selena frowned. "I hate to be the downer in the group, but even if you do all this promo, do you honestly think we'll have that many last-minute travelers?"

Rosie had grappled with the same issue, but she didn't want to get bogged down with negativity. "I don't know. We plan to send personalized emails to anyone who visited our hotel last December and tell them about our holiday offerings. If they book directly with us, they'll get twenty percent off."

"We just need to have a little faith," Charlie said. "Well, faith and hard work. But it'll be worth it if we can keep our jobs."

"Thanks," Rosie said. "Do you want to start us off? What are your favorite ideas?"

Charlie took a swig of her bottled water. "Yes to the festive happy hours on weekday evenings. I talked to Knox about it, and he's on board. Though when I suggested he wear a Santa hat while mixing drinks, he said, 'No way in hell,' which is a darn shame. I might have to work with him on that."

Selena shook her head in amusement. "Twenty bucks says he'll never wear one."

"You're on. I'll bet I can convince him. But let me finish listing my choices." Charlie took another drink and then continued, her voice rising with excitement. "Yes to the family Saturdays with Drew playing Santa, along with cookie decorating and craft stations. Yes to cocoa and caroling, to upping our decorating game in the lobby, and to giving our guests cookies at check-in. That's five, right?"

As the others nodded, Rosie was grateful Charlie had gone first. If they could maintain her level of enthusiasm, they might be able to make this work. Not only that, but it might be fun. She went to the whiteboard and added a checkmark to the ideas Charlie had listed. After they discussed them in terms of feasibility and cost, she called on Selena and then Laurel before sharing her own choices. Just as she was finishing up, a knock came at the door.

"Do you think it's our boss?" Charlie asked. She gathered up her lunch remains and stuffed them in the bag.

"Doubtful. I don't think he'd knock before entering his own conference room." Rosie opened the door to reveal Santa. Or rather, Drew dressed in his Santa attire. The red coat with the white fur trim and black buttons, the matching red pants, the black boots, and the hat. All that was missing was the beard. She stepped back, too overcome to speak.

Even if the suit covered all of him, he was the sexiest Santa she'd ever seen. His red, fur-trimmed pants hugged his butt in a way that was downright sinful.

"Ho, ho, ho, everyone," Drew called out. "Rosie said you were meeting, so I came over to make an in-person plug for Santa. And to bring you caramel brownies." He strode over to the table and placed a glass container on it.

Selena opened the lid and peered inside. "These look homemade. Did you bake them?" She took one out, bit into it, and gave a little moan. "Ohhh. They're so good."

"Thanks, but I can't take the credit. One of my favorite clients made them. They're incredibly decadent, so there's no way I could eat them all myself."

While the others reached for the brownies, Rosie stood in place, still fixated on Drew. All of a sudden, her recent fantasies were a lot easier to envision. Like the one where she was sitting on his lap, naked. Or the even raunchier one where he was bending her over his knee and chastising her for being on the naughty list. Just a light spanking, nothing more, his gloved hand smacking her ass until she mewled with pleasure.

Stop this. You're at work, damn it.

He walked over to her. "I hope it's okay I just showed up. When you told me you were meeting with the Damsels to pick your holiday activities, I thought this would be a fun surprise."

"It is. I mean...you are. I mean. Yes." She swallowed, too tongue-tied to manage a coherent sentence. "You just...um...look really good as Santa. Totally convincing."

"You think so? I'm not even using my special Santa voice." He placed his hands on his hips and spoke in a low rumble. "Have you been a good girl, Rosie Gonzalez?"

Oh, Lord. That deep voice, combined with the twinkle in his eyes, sent her pulse racing. Would he use it on her if they were in bed together? Would he praise her if she did exactly as he said? Just thinking of it sent a surge of desire coursing through her.

"Yes, Santa. I've been a very good girl," she whispered.

That sounded way too flirty. She heard Charlie snicker, then turned to face the Damsels, who were watching them like they were actors in a telenovela.

She needed to get a grip before she made a complete fool of herself. Pushing her lewd thoughts to a dark corner of her brain, she showed Drew the whiteboard. "As you can see from the list, we've narrowed down our favorite options. All of us chose Santa. You'll just need to commit to four Saturday afternoons in December."

He grinned. "No problem. I'll have to tweak my training schedule, but I'll make it work."

"Thanks. I...I mean, *we* really appreciate it."

The door opened abruptly, revealing Preston. As he scanned the room, his gaze landed squarely on Drew. Rosie's heart rate quickened. Would her boss think it unprofessional that "Santa" was hanging out in their conference room?

Preston examined Drew closely. "Is there a reason you're dressed up like Santa Claus?"

"He was auditioning for the role," Rosie said. "For our family

Saturdays at the hotel. He works around the corner at Northlife Fitness but does volunteer gigs as Santa on the weekends."

"He does it for the kids," Charlie said with a touch of pathos. "Isn't that inspiring?"

"You do this voluntarily?" Preston asked. "You're a better man than I am. That suit has to be hot as hell."

Rosie almost laughed out loud. There was no doubt that Drew was hot in that suit, but not in the way Preston was suggesting.

"I don't mind wearing it," Drew said. "Not if it makes kids happy. But right now, I should be getting back to my day job. Please keep me in mind for the role of Santa."

Rosie was grateful he was playing along. "Thanks for coming by, Mr. Richardson. We'll be in touch about the Santa gig."

"Thank you, Miss Gonzalez. I look forward to hearing from you."

She heard the soft muffle of Charlie's laughter but ignored it. After Drew left, she turned to Preston with a bright smile on her face. "Would you like me to present our suggestions? Once we have your approval, we can set our plans in motion."

"Certainly. I like this take-charge attitude of yours." He sat down and took a brownie from the container. "Go ahead. I'm eager to hear what you ladies have come up with."

Rosie let out a relieved breath. If they could make this work, they just might be able to save their jobs.

Seven

After leaving the Duchess, Drew sprinted over to Northlife Fitness and ducked into the back entrance of the gym. Once inside the staff locker room, he leaned against the wall, took off his Santa hat, and wiped the sweat from his forehead.

What were you thinking?

Being around Rosie had short-circuited his brain. First, he'd offered to be her pretend boyfriend, and now he'd shown up at her workplace dressed as Santa. Which might have been appropriate if it was December, but Christmas was still seven weeks away.

To be fair, when he and Rosie had talked on the phone last night, she'd jokingly suggested Santa pop into today's lunch meeting. Like an idiot, he'd taken her idea to heart. Her boss's sudden appearance had thrown him for a loop. Good thing Rosie had been able to handle the situation professionally.

Just as well since her initial reaction to "Santa" hadn't exactly been professional. Maybe Drew was projecting his own feelings, but the longing in her eyes had made him suspect she harbored some naughty thoughts about Santa. And when she said she'd been a "very good girl" in that soft, sultry manner, he'd struggled to control his reaction. It wouldn't do for Santa to have a hard-on.

His phone buzzed with a text from his boss, Mario Bonetti—known to everyone as Bones.

> Bones: Whenever you're free, stop by my office.

> Drew: Sure. Be there in a few minutes.

Normally his boss wasn't the type to call anyone in for a casual chat, but maybe he wanted to discuss the December schedule. In anticipation of his Santa gigs, Drew had asked if he could switch to half days on the weekends. He changed into a compression shirt and gray sweatpants, left the locker room, and headed up to Bones' office, located on the second floor. The door was open, so he poked his head in.

"Hey there. You wanted to talk to me?"

"Come on in." Bones was at his desk. Though he was nearly sixty, he was still in extraordinary shape and rarely missed his daily workout. In his day, he'd won weight-lifting competitions all over Canada.

Drew plunked down on the chair facing Bones' desk. "Is this about next month's schedule? I might have to shift a few clients, but I don't think it should be a problem."

His boss gave a dismissive wave. "Don't worry about it. You know how December is. Everyone's busy with the holidays. As long as you pull your weight in January, we'll be fine."

January was always their busiest month, when they were flooded with new members intent on tackling their New Year's resolutions.

Bones continued. "I wanted to let you know Jared's leaving. He's moving up to Nanaimo to be the assistant manager of a new branch of Northlife that's opening in January."

Jared was leaving? Drew could barely contain his glee. Right from the start, he'd never liked the guy. And when he'd discovered Jared and Evelyn were hooking up on the sly, he'd hated him even more. "Already? He's only been here since May."

"Apparently, he and Evelyn are looking to buy a house once they get married. Nanaimo's a little more affordable."

"Makes sense. I think everywhere on Vancouver Island is more affordable than Victoria." While Drew had no desire to move, he could see the appeal. Nanaimo was a beautiful coastal city, located about an hour and a half north of Victoria. "I assume Evelyn's leaving, too?"

"That's the plan. Her last day is December thirtieth. I'll be sad to lose her."

"But not Jared, I take it?"

Bones laughed. "Do you even have to ask?"

Though he was the one who'd hired Jared to take on the role of fitness manager—a position that placed him in charge of all the personal trainers—the two of them had clashed almost immediately. Bones believed fitness was for everyone, whereas Jared only liked working with people who were already in decent shape. Due to his disdain for the gym's elderly clientele, the Golden Oldies couldn't stand him.

Drew felt like celebrating. Working at the gym would be infinitely more enjoyable if he didn't have to report directly to Jared. Having Evelyn gone made the deal even sweeter.

"Thanks for letting me know. If you need me to take on any of Jared's clients, I can start in January."

"Actually, I was wondering if you'd consider applying for his job."

"Me?" Even when the position had come open last spring, he hadn't pursued it. Which had led to Bones hiring Jared, who'd subsequently upended Drew's world.

"Why not?" Bones asked. "You've been with us for five years, and you're one of the most popular trainers here. Your clients love you, there's always a waiting list for your boot camp classes, and your reviews are consistently high."

"Thanks." Drew loved what he did, but a little validation never hurt. "The thing is—I don't have any management experience, other than a few business classes."

"There's not much to it. You'd be supervising the other trainers, so there'd be some paperwork, but you'd still get to spend time on the floor. The job comes with a higher salary and better benefits. It wouldn't hurt to consider your long-term goals and decide what you want for the future."

Right now, Drew wanted to keep doing exactly what he'd done for the past five years: teach group exercise classes, train clients, and coach people on fitness and nutrition. But was he being too shortsighted? "Can I think about it?"

"Sure. Just don't take too long. If you're not interested, I'll open it up to the other trainers. But you'd be my first choice."

"I appreciate it."

"Good. You also emailed me last week about some new boot camp ideas?"

"Yeah, I was thinking of starting one that incorporates more team challenges because the added incentive makes people try a little harder." With Bones' encouragement, he went on to elaborate. Fitness was an industry where you could always keep learning, so he spent a lot of his free time doing research: watching videos, reading articles, and chatting online with trainers from gyms all over Canada.

As he left the office, Bones' offer lingered in the back of his mind. Should he be thinking about the future? By not pursuing a management role, was he coasting through life without challenging himself?

He needed to ask someone for advice. Though he had no doubt his fellow trainers would support him, they wouldn't understand his anxiety over taking on the role. And right now, his older sister, Kate, would be busy teaching preschool.

For a second, he was tempted to call his mom. But his parents had never supported his career. He could still remember the way they'd reacted when he'd come home for the summer after his first year at the University of Victoria. With pride, he'd told them that he'd decided to gear his studies toward landing a job in the fitness industry.

His mom had regarded him with disbelief. "Are you shitting me? You're paying good money to take gym classes?"

"That's not all I'm doing," he said. "I'll be learning how the human body works. Studying subjects like anatomy, physiology, and kinesiology."

"Then you should be getting a medical degree," his dad said. "That way, you could make real money instead of being an underpaid gym rat."

Never mind that a medical degree would mean more years of school and thousands more dollars. "This is what I'm passionate about," he said. "For once, it would be nice to have your support."

"If by support, you mean money, then you're shit out of luck," his dad said. "You're paying for all of it yourself."

Like he hadn't been doing that already? His parents hadn't put a dime toward helping him or his sister attend university. "I'm fine with that."

His mom snorted in derision. "You'd better be. Thanks to your dumb-ass father and his idiotic attempt at accounting, we're still paying off a huge tax bill."

And just like that, his parents were at each other's throats, revisiting the same time-worn arguments they'd had for years.

A rough voice jolted him from his memories. "Drew? You okay?"

He startled, then turned to face one of his coworkers, who was standing at his locker, retrieving a gym bag. "Sorry. Did you ask me something?"

"You were spacing out just now. You good?"

"Yeah, I'm good."

Enough wallowing. For now, he had to focus on today's clients.

But if he had the chance, he'd call Rosie later and ask her opinion about Bones' offer.

HIS LAST CLIENT OF THE DAY WAS HANNAH, THE DE facto leader of the Golden Oldies. At age seventy-eight, she was still in remarkable shape and rarely missed a workout. Usually she scheduled her sessions in the afternoons when the gym was less crowded, but due to a conflict, she'd switched to a later time slot.

Unfortunately, at six thirty on a weeknight, Northlife Fitness was buzzing with activity. Over in one corner, the teens attending Jared's speed training class were doing sprints on the gym's track. Most of the machines were in use. Classic rock blared from the speakers, and a Montreal Canadiens game played on the big-screen TVs. Drew had carved out a space for Hannah on one of the mats so they could work on her kettlebell routine.

"Just ten more reps left," he said now. "You're doing great."

She went on to do twenty, which was typical of her. When she was done, she turned to him with a sly smile. "That young lady's got her eye on you."

He chuckled. Ever since Evelyn had dumped him, Hannah had taken it upon herself to find him a new girlfriend. "Which young lady?"

"Over there by the lat pull-down machine. I caught her staring at you three times."

He followed Hannah's gaze. To his surprise, Rosie stood beside the machine, wiping it down with a towel. His mouth went dry at the sight of her sexy curves, accentuated by her black crop top and bike shorts. Before he could turn away, she caught his eye and waved at him. He beckoned her over.

She approached him and Hannah. "Hi, Drew."

"Hey, Rosie. You came back. I thought you were going to wait until January."

"Even if I'm busy, I figured I can squeeze in one or two workouts a week." She smiled at Hannah. "Sorry to interrupt your session with Drew. I just wanted to say hi."

"I noticed you staring at him, missy. Why not ask him out? He's single, you know." Hannah was nothing if not blunt.

Rosie's eyes sparkled with affection. "Didn't he tell you? We're together."

Though she'd tossed the words out casually, hearing them was a balm to Drew's soul. Knowing Hannah, she'd share this news with the other members of the Golden Oldies, which meant everyone at the gym would know about it in a few days' time.

Hannah harrumphed. "Drew Richardson. You never breathed a word, even when Maribeth tried to set you up with her granddaughter last week. If you have a girlfriend this lovely, you need to show her off."

"I like the way you think," Rosie said to her. "It was nice meeting you, but I'll let you get back to your workout."

"Wait," Drew said. Maybe he was being greedy, but he wanted more time with her than just a quick interaction at the gym. "After you're done, do you want to get a drink? Or some hot chocolate?"

"Hot chocolate sounds marvelous. Could we meet up in a half hour? I need to finish on the weight machines and grab a shower."

"Perfect. I'll meet you at the smoothie bar."

As she walked away, he stared at her ass. Clad in black spandex, it was far too tempting.

Hannah harrumphed again. "Save it for later, lover boy. I want to finish up before I'm in the grave."

"Sorry," he said. "Let's move on to the exercise ball."

For the rest of Hannah's workout, his focus was off. To make up for it, he promised to comp her an extra session. She dismissed him with a smile and told him to have fun with his girlfriend.

His girlfriend.

Even if it wasn't real, he liked the sound of it.

Eight

Rosie and Drew ended up at Alma's Beanery, a local coffeehouse a block away from Northlife Fitness. One thing Rosie loved about downtown Victoria was how walkable it was. The streets near the harbor were lined with gift shops, restaurants, pubs, and coffeehouses. Some areas, like Bastion Square—home to a popular artisan market—and the tourist-friendly parts of Government Street, were pedestrian-only. Unfortunately, tonight's weather was so rainy that she and Drew were forced to make a mad dash from the gym to Alma's.

After ordering hot chocolate, they settled into a couple of armchairs. Outside, the driving rain pattered against the windows, making their surroundings even cozier. Across from her, Drew looked as irresistible as ever, wearing a red fleece hoodie and gray sweatpants, his hair still damp from the shower. Thanks to her recent Santa fantasies, she was gripped with the urge to curl up on his lap and rest her head against his shoulder.

Which, obviously, wasn't going to happen.

But when he placed his hand on her knee—just the slightest of touches—a little shiver danced along her spine.

"Thanks for coming to the gym today," he said. "And for telling Hannah about us."

The appreciation in his voice warmed her even more than the piping-hot cocoa. "My pleasure. It's fun playing the role of your girlfriend. But tonight's workout might come back to bite me in the butt. It's been a while since I worked some of those muscles."

"Make sure to stretch properly. Do you have a yoga app?"

"I still do, thanks to the one you recommended last year. And while we're thanking each other, I wanted to tell you what an outstanding job you did on Sunday night. Five stars."

"Do you think your mom liked me?" he asked. "She hugged me before I left."

He sounded so vulnerable that she was glad she didn't have to lie. "My mom adored you. Trust me, she doesn't give out leftovers to just anybody. My dad was impressed, too. He texted me afterward and called you a 'fine young man.' He never said that about my ex."

No surprise, given that the one time she'd brought Erik to Sunday dinner, he'd barely touched the food. Later, he'd said to her, "I'm just not a big fan of Mexican cooking. It's so heavy and fattening, you know?"

Heavy or not, it was the food she'd grown up with, and he hadn't made an effort.

"I'm glad Sunday was a success," Drew said. "But I hope I didn't screw up things with your boss today. When I crashed your meeting, I didn't think he'd be there."

"It was fine. He believed you were auditioning for the role of Santa." She gave a little snort. "Of course, I didn't tell him you were the *only* contender."

"How did the rest of the meeting go?" He licked a dollop of whipped cream off his cocoa, which drew attention to his full lips. Rosie squirmed inwardly, trying hard not to imagine those lips claiming hers in a passionate kiss.

"It went well," she said. "Preston was on board with all the ideas we picked, as long as we can keep our costs down. Even though it's going to be a ton of extra work, I love seeing a plan take shape, especially with such a supportive team on my side."

By the time her boss had left, she'd felt confident that she and the Damsels had set up a series of manageable goals. What was more, they were excited about them.

"Do you like being in management?" Drew asked. "Or does it stress you out?"

The question took her aback, but maybe he wanted to understand what she was dealing with. "A little of both? I'd feel better about my job if it wasn't in jeopardy right now or if the Duchess wasn't struggling to survive, but I like my role at the hotel. And I definitely prefer it to working the front desk."

"Even if it's way more challenging?"

"Yeah. Maybe I'm a little too driven, but I love a good challenge," she said. "Why? Are you thinking of getting into management at the gym?"

As he told her about his meeting with Bones and the offer he'd gotten, she was pleased he felt comfortable enough to confide in her. When he was done, he asked her what she thought.

"Personally, I think it's a great opportunity," she said. "But only if it's what you want. Are you happy where you are?"

"Pretty much, yeah. I love what I do. But money-wise, it would make sense to move up the ladder. I'm doing okay, but I barely have any savings. I'd like to build up a cushion in case I get injured or laid off. I never want to end up like my parents—broke and miserable and hating each other because of it."

This was the second time he'd disparaged his parents. She could have let it go, but since he seemed willing to open up, she decided to delve a little deeper. "What's the deal with your folks? If you'd rather not talk about it, I understand, but I'm here to listen."

He didn't respond right away, which made her worry she'd pushed him too far. But after he finished his cocoa and set it on the table beside them, he spoke up. "You sure you don't mind? I usually don't burden people with this shit."

"I don't mind at all." If anything, she wanted to know him better. For as many conversations as they'd had at the gym, they'd often been surface-level, chatting about movies, exchanging gossip about their jobs, and teasing each other playfully.

"The short version? They're messed up. They weren't always that bad. When I was a kid, they took me and my sister on these killer camping trips. We couldn't afford much else, but those trips had a big impact on me. That's why I love the outdoors so much. When I was eleven, they invested in a kayak rental business in Cowichan Bay. They partnered with a friend of theirs and sunk their savings into it, but that asshole ran off with all the money. A year later, they went out of business and ended up in debt. We had to sell our house and move into a crappy apartment. From then on, we were pretty much broke."

"God, Drew, I'm so sorry." What an awful way to grow up.

"That's not the worst part. Sometimes when families don't have much, they rally together. Not my folks. They started blaming each other, and it just got worse. It would have been better if they'd gotten divorced, but they were both too stubborn. So, they've spent years tearing each other down. That's why I hate going home for Christmas."

She wanted to curse them out for putting Drew through hell, but succumbing to a rant wouldn't solve anything. Instead, she'd try to give him the support he needed.

"I'm sorry you had to deal with that. It's so unfair. But, to your other question, if you're worried about saving money, then the management job seems like a smart move. Unless you're nervous about taking the next step. Which is understandable since you'd be dealing with a whole new level of responsibility."

Last year, when she'd been offered the role of assistant manager at the hotel, her excitement had been tempered with anxiety over the thought of proving herself worthy.

"A part of me would like to stay where I am because I'm good at it," he said. "If I try something new, I might fail miserably. My parents did that, and it destroyed their lives."

"But you're not them. You've got friends in your corner, and I'm sure the other trainers would support you." She gave him a wry smile. "Maybe not Evelyn, but she'll be gone soon."

"When the job came open last time, she pushed me to take it. I told her I wasn't ready for that kind of challenge, which was probably a big mistake since Jared was hired to fill the position." He gave a harsh laugh. "Then he went after Evelyn."

What a dick. Even if she'd never met him, Rosie knew his type. "He sounds like a jerk."

"Pretty much. From day one, he rubbed me the wrong way. Super arrogant and dismissive. And definitely more ambitious than me. That's one of the reasons Evelyn went back to him. I just wasn't enough for her."

Fighting back her anger—at Jared, Evelyn, and Drew's parents —Rosie reached over and took his hand. "That's her loss. Don't let anyone tell you that you aren't enough. You're one of the sweetest, most wonderful guys I know. I'm lucky to have you as a friend."

When he regarded her with tenderness, it was all she could do not to give him the biggest hug ever. But if she did that, she was afraid she'd cross the line from friendship into something more intimate.

"Thanks," he murmured. "You're pretty great yourself. I hope last Sunday's dinner made you feel like you're enough, too."

"It did. It also made me realize I might have been projecting my own insecurities onto my family. Yes, they're critical, but they're also looking out for me." For months now, she hadn't been able to see this. But Drew's presence had given her a new perspective. "They didn't want Erik to screw me over—which he totally did—and they don't want me getting screwed over by the Duchess, either. Even if I can't ease up on my workload, I can accept their help. Thanks for getting them on board with the holiday ideas."

"I didn't do that much, but I'll take the credit." He grinned. "When's our next dinner?"

"November eighteenth—if you're available."

"I'll make sure of it. Thanks for going along with this dating scheme. And for listening to me tonight."

"It's my pleasure."

She meant it. Even if she'd been a little skeptical of his ruse at first, it was working out just the way he'd suggested. The two of them, teaming up together to get through the holidays, offering each other support and friendship. Already, she was in a better frame of mind than she'd been last week.

But she also knew it would be far too easy to delude herself that this friendship could lead to romance. For that reason, she couldn't get in much deeper.

AFTER WALKING ROSIE TO HER CAR, DREW HEADED back to Northlife Fitness. He still had to fill out his gym log and check tomorrow's schedule. At eight thirty, the place was pretty empty, all the group fitness classes done for the night. A few of the treadmills were occupied, as were some of the weight machines, but that was it.

He jogged upstairs to the small office shared by the trainers and logged on to the staff computer. As he was pulling up his account, his phone buzzed with a text from his sister, Kate. He'd left her a message about Bones' offer but hadn't been sure if he'd hear from her tonight since she had a book club meeting.

> Kate: You can call anytime. I couldn't deal with book club.

Immediately, his Spidey senses started tingling. Though Kate was an extrovert—she had to be, given that she was part-owner of a preschool and taught most of the 4K classes there—she was also given to bouts of depression in which she abruptly withdrew from all her planned social activities. He always worried when that happened.

He punched in her number. "Hey, Kate. You doing okay?"

She responded with a weary sigh. "Hey, bud. I'm not at my best. I should have read the blurb before diving into this book. Then I would have found out it's about a woman who had a super-dysfunctional childhood. Naturally, she overcame it, but only after dealing with a bunch of emotional abuse. I hate that shit."

Ugh. Too close to home. "Sorry. Maybe you should stick with romance."

"No kidding. Either that or mysteries. These weepy memoirs are the worst."

"Do you need me to stop by?" Even if he was tired, he'd make time for her. He always did.

"Nope. I'm good. Just curling up with a bowl of oatmeal and rewatching the third season of *Bridgerton*. It's still as swoony as ever."

It was beyond weird to him that his sister's comfort food was oatmeal, as opposed to ice cream or pie, but whatever worked. "Anything else bugging you?"

"Just Mom. She called about some stupid shit. Her Wi-Fi was out, and I tried to help her fix it over the phone. But then I realized why it wasn't working."

Drew slumped down in his seat. "Let me guess. She didn't pay the bill?"

"Yep. She had it on auto-pay, but her account was overdrawn." She sighed again. "Please don't let me end up like her."

"You won't, I promise." The only upside of having financially screwed-up parents was that he and Kate were incredibly careful with money.

"Hey, tell me what's going on with this job thing. And the Rosie stuff. Are you actually dating again?"

Over the past few days, he'd been so busy that he'd only left Kate a series of messages. But he hadn't said much about Rosie because their fake-dating agreement was too hard to explain via text. The fewer people who knew the truth about it, the better, but he couldn't lie to his sister. They'd always been honest with each other, and he valued her opinion.

When he was done telling her about it, she started laughing. "Holy shit. What a total screw-you to Evelyn. Did you tell her you were dating someone new?"

He frowned, remembering his ex's reaction. "Yeah, but she wasn't that jealous. If anything, she was all, 'don't hurt Rosie the way you hurt me,' which is bullshit."

"Total bullshit," Kate agreed. "I'll bet she was just covering up. She's probably mad that you're not moping over her anymore."

"Maybe. I'm just glad I won't have to feel like a loser when I go to her wedding. It might even be fun." He let his mind drift, imagining Rosie on his arm, wearing a stylish cocktail dress and heels, her thick, dark hair falling loose to her shoulders.

"Good. When do I get to meet her? Can I pop by the hotel sometime?"

"Absolutely. I also volunteered your help in preparing the crafts for their family Saturday event. If you're free that day, you could come in and assist them. I'm sure Rosie would love it."

Drew suspected the two women would hit it off since they were both so empathetic. Like Rosie, Kate truly cared about the people she worked with.

After filling her in on his dinner with Rosie's family, he told her about the job offer from Bones. She was just as encouraging as Rosie had been, especially since she knew how much he worried about building up his savings. Neither of them ever wanted to end up in a huge financial hole.

By the time he was done chatting with her, he felt confident she'd be okay. He left her to finish up her episode of *Bridgerton* and filled in his gym log for the day. As he was about to leave, he saw he'd missed a text from Rosie.

> Rosie: Thanks for the cocoa. I'm glad we got to talk. I'm planning to come to the gym on Thursday after work. Will you be there?

A simple question, but it made his heart swell with happiness.

> Drew: I'll make sure of it. See you then.

> Rosie: See you. Good night, Drew.

> Drew: Night, Rosie.

As he set down the phone, the warmth built up inside of him, like a tiny, glowing sun. Even if he and Rosie were only *pretending* to date, their friendship felt very real. Not that he'd dare wade in too much further. While he was grateful they could offer each other support and encouragement, anything more was a risk he wasn't willing to take.

Nine

28 DAYS UNTIL CHRISTMAS

Rosie stumbled into work, cursing the fact that it was still dark out. At this hour, none of the nearby coffee shops were open, so she'd been forced to brew a cup at home. If she had time later, she'd replenish it with a latte from Alma's.

With four weeks to go until Christmas, Charlie had suggested they get started on decorating the hotel. Though no one was excited about arriving at work before sunrise, they'd all agreed to come in extra early.

Upon reaching the front desk, Rosie was pleased to see the night shift clerks had already started decorating. Clad in Santa hats, they were busy arranging twinkling lights and garlands around the check-in area, as well as setting up signs advertising the hotel's upcoming events, including the festive weeknight happy hours and the family Saturdays.

Rosie set a tin on the counter. "Looking good. These are Mexican wedding cookies from my sister. You can tuck them behind the desk for later."

One of the clerks smiled at her. "Thanks. Did you see the tree Charlie brought in? It's gorgeous."

When Rosie focused her gaze on the lobby, located just to the right of the front desk, her jaw dropped. Standing beside the inlaid tile fireplace was a stunning, eight-foot-tall tree, adorned with a rainbow of vintage glass ornaments, beaded garlands, and frosted lights.

Charlie peeked out from behind the tree. "Behold! Isn't it glorious?"

Rosie walked over to her. "It's amazing. This must have taken you hours to set up. I hope you didn't spend all night here."

Charlie laughed. "Nope. All I did was haul it over this morning, as is. My mom uses this bougie service to prep her house for the holidays. Last year, her decorator went all-in on the vintage look, but now that style is passé. I was able to grab this tree from our garage before Mom tossed it out."

Rosie couldn't imagine her parents swapping out their family's Christmas decorations just because they were outdated. Among her favorites were the colorful tin ornaments that her grandparents had brought from Mexico sixty years ago.

"What's the new style this year?" she asked.

"All the ornaments are dark blue and silver. Kind of a night sky vibe, I guess." Charlie shrugged. "Anyway, Knox helped me bring the tree in his truck, along with a bunch of other decorations."

Knox came through the entrance of the hotel, pushing a luggage cart laden with boxes and potted poinsettias. He parked it beside the tree. "Here's the rest of the stuff."

Rosie couldn't help but grin. "Morning, Knox. I've never seen you here this early."

He busied himself unloading the boxes. "Yeah, well, I figured I'd pitch in. I don't want anyone getting canned because this place isn't festive enough. I'm gonna make some coffee. Is the breakfast room open?"

"Not yet. The kitchen staff doesn't start prepping until six, but you can use my key card." Rosie handed it to him. "Thanks. I appreciate it."

"No problem," he muttered.

As he ambled off, Rosie nudged Charlie. "Knox isn't a morning person. There's no way he would have done that for anyone except you."

"Nope. He was doing it for the good of the hotel."

Rosie smirked. "Right. You keep telling yourself that." She went to help Selena, who had just emerged from the elevator bearing an overloaded luggage cart. "You doing okay?"

Selena scowled. "It's 5:00 a.m. How could I possibly be okay? Remind me again why we're decorating so early? And doing it ourselves instead of hiring professionals?"

"We wanted to set up the lobby before people came down for breakfast," Charlie said. "This way, it's more like a magical surprise."

"And we didn't hire a decorating service because our budget is so paltry," Rosie added. Last week, she'd asked Preston if they could free up the funds to hire someone, but he hadn't budged. Instead, he'd told her, "I'm sure you and your staff can pull something together."

Then, when she'd invited him to join this morning's decorating party, he'd passed, claiming he didn't want to derail his exercise routine. Yet another response that had her wishing he'd make a little more effort.

Selena pointed to the boxes. "This is half the stuff from our storage area—mostly decorations for the breakfast room. I'm not sure if it's all usable."

"Do you want to take it over there and start going through it?" Rosie asked. "Knox is already brewing coffee."

"Sounds good. Laurel should be up soon with the other boxes."

Once Selena headed off, Rosie turned to Charlie. "What else do we need to set up?"

"There's an antique sled and a bunch of wrapped presents in these boxes that we can put under the tree. I also bought extra paper in case we need to rewrap any of the gifts. Some of them might be torn or faded."

As Rosie helped Charlie arrange the presents, she began perking up. Even if she hadn't wanted to get up at four this morning, she couldn't deny the hotel was already looking festive. Maybe now when guests walked in, they wouldn't notice the faded carpeting or the scuffed counter at the front desk; instead, they'd focus on all the lights and the colorful tree in the lobby.

"Coming in early to decorate was a stroke of brilliance," she said to Charlie. "Not gonna lie, I was cursing you when my alarm went off, but I'm starting to get that holiday feeling."

"You see? All we've done for the past three weeks is plan, but now we get to watch it all take shape. You should enjoy it."

"I want to, but I'm a little worried. Laurel's marketing team is going full steam ahead, but our occupancy rate has barely risen."

Every night, when Rosie reviewed the hotel's numbers, her heart sank a little. She wanted so badly for their plans to succeed, but so far, they hadn't received a lot of additional bookings for December.

Charlie set another poinsettia next to the tree. "I don't get it. We're trying so hard to make the Duchess sound appealing. Did you see all the content Laurel's intern has been posting on TikTok and Instagram? It's super creative."

"Yeah, and her posts have gotten a ton of views. The problem is—we started this so late. Most of the people who'll be traveling in December probably made their plans back in the fall."

"Maybe the weekday happy hours will help. Knox put together a list of holiday-themed cocktails, and they sound *so* good." Charlie rubbed her hands together in anticipation. "I can't wait to try them."

At six thirty, when they were almost done, Drew walked into the lobby carrying two boxes of donuts from Tim Hortons. "Good morning! I come bearing donuts."

As tired as she was, Rosie brightened at his appearance. By

now, they'd been "together" for almost four weeks, but she still lit up every time she saw him.

"Hey, there," she said. "Isn't it against your fitness rules to be bringing us donuts?"

"What can I say? I love a good donut as much as anyone else." He glanced at the tree. "Whoa. You guys did an amazing job. Those old-school glass ornaments are so cool."

"You don't think they're passé?" Charlie teased.

"Is that even a thing when it comes to Christmas? Not at all. They're great."

"Let's dart into the breakfast room real quick," Rosie said. "That way, we can enjoy some coffee with our donuts before we have to open the room for guests at seven."

"Sounds good," Drew said. "I'm gonna give the front desk clerks first pick."

As he strolled over to the check-in area with his boxes of donuts, Charlie smirked at Rosie. "Speaking of going the extra mile, it's sweet that your 'boyfriend' showed up early with treats for everyone."

A warm flush crept up Rosie's cheeks. "I didn't expect it, but it's very sweet."

"Things are going well otherwise? With the fake dating?"

Rosie piled the empty boxes onto the luggage cart. "Really well. Every time I go to the gym, he seems pumped to see me. I flirt with him and call him adorable pet names, and sometimes we get smoothies after. Though last night, we went to Noodlebox and had a late dinner."

"I love that place. Their kung pao box is *so* good."

"It's the best. We got into this intense discussion about the Bond movies. I still can't believe he prefers Sean Connery when Daniel Craig is unequivocally the hottest Bond ever." Seeing that Charlie was staring her down, she stopped. "What?"

"How can you not see how perfect Drew is? This is more than a faux romance."

Rosie shook her head emphatically. "No, it's not. We're just friends, that's all. Good friends who like the same kind of movies, and like to hang out together, and um..." She groaned. "I'm doing a crappy job convincing you, aren't I?"

"Totally crappy. It's okay if you like him as more than a friend. I just don't want you to get hurt."

"I won't. If anything, work's going to get more intense once our holiday activities start on December first. All the more reason I wouldn't want to deal with the demands of a real romantic relationship. I'd feel so guilty about neglecting him."

Even as she said it, she knew it wasn't quite the truth. So far, Drew hadn't complained about her schedule. He'd just been happy to see her whenever she could fit him in. Like last week, when she'd joined him at the gym for the surprise bridal shower that the staff had thrown for Jared and Evelyn. She'd expected Drew to struggle with it, but he'd made teasing asides to her the entire time. Afterward, they'd gone out for drinks at a nearby pub and kicked ass at the pub's weekly trivia night.

Drew walked back to them. "Should we cruise over to the breakfast room for our donut break? Rosie, I got your favorite kind—Boston Cream. Actually, I got you two. One for now, and one for later, in case you need a sugar fix."

"Aww, that's so thoughtful," Charlie said. "You almost make me believe that you and Rosie are really together."

"I know, right?" he said. "Plus, we're having a blast doing it."

As he headed toward the breakfast room, Charlie lowered her voice and addressed Rosie. "Too bad it's not real."

Too bad, indeed.

Ten

By the time December arrived, Rosie was spending all her spare time at the Duchess. Early mornings, late nights, weekends, whatever it took. Today, her anxiety was higher than usual because the hotel was hosting their first "family Saturday." Since she hadn't asked guests to register for the event ahead of time, she didn't know how many people to expect. At least twenty families with small children were currently staying at the Duchess, but they might have other plans.

She'd arrived at the hotel at ten, fully intending to help the Damsels set up, but due to an unexpected glitch in their central reservation system, she'd spent an hour dealing with IT. Then, while waiting for the system to come back online, she'd had to help the front desk deal with reservation requests and checkouts. By the time the crisis was resolved, she had less than twenty minutes before their family event was due to start. She hustled over to the breakfast room, grateful to see all the Damsels there, along with Laurel's intern and three high school students, who were acting as "helper elves."

Charlie ran over to Rosie. "Thank God you're here. Is the front desk back online yet?"

"It is now," Rosie said. "Thanks for getting everything ready."

"No problem," Charlie said. "I'm so nervous. What if no one shows up?"

A queasy sensation settled in the pit of Rosie's stomach. Given Charlie's perpetual optimism, her anxiety wasn't a good sign. "What makes you think no one's coming?"

"I don't know." Charlie twisted her hands together. "This morning's IT outage made me anxious. Like, maybe the universe isn't smiling on us. And it's pouring rain outside."

"Here I thought *I* was the pessimist," Selena said. "Personally, I think we lucked out with the weather. With all this rain, families will be looking for things to do indoors."

"Plus, the marketing team did everything they could to promote today's event," Laurel added. "The *Times Colonist* ran a short piece about it yesterday."

"I'm just grateful we've gotten this far," Rosie said. "Why don't you all show me what you've done?" She'd rather focus on their accomplishments than on their fears that the hotel's first family event would be a failure.

Charlie led her to one section of the breakfast room, where the tables were draped in seasonal vinyl tablecloths. "This is the craft corner for kids to make different ornaments."

As Rosie scanned all the supplies—containers of Popsicle sticks, markers, cotton balls, beads, buttons, ribbons, and felt—she hoped Charlie hadn't spent too much. "Wow. Where'd you get all this stuff?"

"Most of it came from Drew's sister, Kate. She was going to help us out today, but she already had plans. So, last week, when you had to attend that motivational seminar with Preston, she stopped by and dropped off everything. We totally bonded." Charlie showed her another table. "This one's for the gingerbread people, plus icing and candy for decorating them. I can't believe how many you made."

"Most of the credit goes to Isabella. She organized all of it and invited our cousins to help." Thanks to Rosie's sister, the cookie-baking session had turned into an impromptu holiday party, complete with tunes, cocktails, and gossip.

Laurel joined them and pointed to the buffet station that ran along one side of the room. "In case anyone needs refreshments, we've got plenty of snacks: peppermint bark, bags of white chocolate pretzels, candy canes, and three kinds of Christmas cookies, plus we set up a hot cocoa dispenser and two carafes of coffee."

"And..." Charlie gestured to a tall photo booth in the corner. "Ta-da! Selena got this at half price. Look at all the fun props!" She held up a giant gingerbread man.

Selena gave them a smug smile. "The breakfast cook's brother runs a party rental place. He gave me a great deal." Next to the photo booth was a box of light-up necklaces. She grabbed one and slipped it over Rosie's head. "There. Now you look more festive."

Rosie's throat swelled up with emotion. She'd known about most of their activities, but the photo booth was a wonderful surprise. "Thanks. You've all done such a great job. I talked to Preston earlier, and he's going to stop by in a bit."

"What about Drew?" Selena asked. "When's he coming?"

"He'll be here at three thirty, dressed in his full Santa outfit." Hopefully, by then, they'd have enough kids in attendance to justify his presence.

"We've got Santa's area all roped off." Laurel led her to a corner of the room where a handmade sign reading, "Welcome to the North Pole," stood next to a wooden throne lined with plush red cushions. "The set director of VOS Musical Theatre loaned me this throne. It's from their fall production of the musical *Camelot*."

"I love it," Rosie said. "Thanks, everyone. I know this has been a ton of work."

"Make sure you thank Drew for pitching in as Santa," Selena added. "And I'm talking a real thank-you, not a sisterly hug."

Heat bloomed in Rosie's cheeks. "We're only pretending to date, remember?"

"So you say, but you've been hanging out with him a lot."

Rosie nodded, not wanting to admit the depth of her feelings out loud. Even as her work life grew increasingly demanding, Drew's presence helped keep her spirits up. The more time she spent with him, the more she wanted to date him for real.

But it wasn't an option. He hadn't hinted—not once—that he wanted more from her than friendship and a fake girlfriend. Not only was he still recovering from Evelyn's betrayal, but his issues also went much deeper. Every time he opened up about his dysfunctional parents, Rosie's heart ached for him.

When a knock came at the door, she went to answer it, hoping Preston hadn't decided to pop by early. She didn't want him to show up until a few families were in attendance.

A petite Latina woman with wildly curly hair and a huge smile greeted her. "Hey, there! Are you Rosalina?"

"Just Rosie, thanks. And you're...Sofia?" Last week, she'd gotten a message from Sofia—a popular food and travel influencer who'd decided to visit the hotel. Though Sofia had arrived last night, Rosie hadn't gotten the chance to meet her yet.

"Yep. Sofia Sanchez. Better known by my handle, SoFood SoFia. I was psyched when Isabella reached out to me and said you needed help."

"You're friends with my sister?" When Isabella had mentioned she "knew" a few influencers, Rosie had assumed she followed them online, not that she was at their level.

"I've never met Isabella in real life, but she's one of my favorite Latina mommy influencers on TikTok. Her videos are so insightful. And they're funny, too." Sofia patted her stomach, which showed the smallest hint of a baby bump. "I started following her when I found out I was expecting. I'm due in April, and I'm over the moon about it, except for the part where I can't indulge in any holiday cocktails."

Since when was Isabella a TikTok sensation? Rosie couldn't believe she hadn't heard about this. Maybe it was time she paid more attention to her family rather than just complaining about them.

"Congratulations on the baby," she said to Sofia. "Our bartender can make you a holiday mocktail if you want."

"Maybe later, thanks. Gotta say, Isabella's invite came out of the blue. I usually like to plan a few months ahead, but my husband and I were already traveling to Seattle so that he could give a talk on Maya settlement patterns at the University of Washington. He's an archaeologist. Like Indiana Jones, but way hotter." She laughed. "Anyway, since your sister said you'd comp our stay, I figured why not extend our trip? So, we took the ferry here from Seattle."

"Thanks for coming. I really appreciate it." With rooms going empty, offering social media influencers free lodging was a no-brainer, especially if they could boost the hotel's visibility.

"No problem. Victoria looks like a gorgeous city." Sofia glanced around the breakfast room. "When do the families get here?"

"Very soon, I hope," Rosie said. "This is our first time doing the event, so I'm not sure how well attended it will be."

"That's okay. I'll do what I can. Take some video footage, talk up the hotel and its history. I did a little research, and it looked incredible in the 1920s. A total Great Gatsby vibe."

Rosie sighed. "It was impressive in its heyday. Now—not so much."

"Yeah, not gonna lie, my room feels outdated. The carpeting is worn, and the décor is kinda meh. But I'll play up the good stuff. Don't you worry." She peeked over at the snack table. "I'm gonna grab a few cookies. Now that I'm in my second trimester, I'm hungry all the time."

No matter how today went, Rosie would have to thank her sister. For all of Isabella's teasing and nagging, she'd really come through. Rosie watched as Sofia flitted around the room, introducing herself to the others and checking out the photo booth.

At two, Rosie unlocked the door. To her relief, three families stood waiting. As she ushered them in, one of the teenage "elves" offered to show the children around. Sofia engaged with the kids immediately, asking them questions about Christmas. Even if no one else showed up, the families in attendance would have a great time.

Over the next twenty minutes, three other families trickled in. Rosie tried to remain optimistic. Six families meant they were off to a good start, but it wouldn't satisfy her boss. She could already imagine the painful apology she'd have to make for not meeting his expectations.

Then, at two thirty, a sizeable clump of people—easily two dozen or more—entered the breakfast room. Charlie spoke under her breath. "Oh my God. The Restalls are here."

"The ones doing that big family reunion?" Rosie asked.

Landing the Restalls had been a huge win. Usually, they stayed at the Grand Duke for their annual reunion, but since it was full, they'd booked rooms at the Duchess instead.

"Yeah. Today's agenda included a carriage ride and a visit to the Butchart Gardens for their Christmas displays. I'm guessing the rain messed up their plans." Charlie walked over to greet them.

Rosie wanted to bust out a celebratory dance. Maybe the Duchess hadn't been the Restalls' first choice, but she could make them feel like they'd made the right decision.

With the deluge of attendees, she and her staff were put to work. She radioed the kitchen to request more cookies, as well as any other snacks they could round up. At this rate, they'd have to restock before next Saturday, but that was a good problem to have.

At three thirty, Charlie told Rosie she would announce Santa's arrival. She called the entire room to attention, then led them in an impromptu sing-along of "Santa Claus is Coming to Town."

When Drew burst into the room, clad in his full regalia—which now included a long white beard—Rosie was once again transfixed at the sight of him. Her knees literally buckled as he cast a grin her way.

How was she lucky enough to be dating the hottest Santa ever?

"Happy December, everyone!" he called out. "I'm thrilled to see so many good boys and girls here."

Rosie wanted to run over and greet him, but she couldn't make herself move. All she could do was stare as her Santa fantasies came back in a rush—including one where he'd stripped off his red suit, one piece at a time, like he was in a Magic Mike revue.

Laurel went over to his side and took his arm. "Hey there, Santa! So glad you could make it here from the North Pole."

"Good thing Canada's pretty close to the Arctic Circle." His eyes twinkled as he smiled at the crowd. "But getting here wasn't easy, since my reindeer prefer traveling in the snow."

Laurel led him over to his corner. "Here you go. We even found a throne for you. I'm going to have the children line up, and then you can talk to them one by one. Is that okay?"

"Certainly!" Drew settled himself on the throne. "I can't wait to get started."

Rosie wondered if he'd ever acted before. Had he done any theatre in high school? How else to explain his complete comfort level in playing Santa? Or—for that matter—the confidence he'd shown when he'd eased into the role of her boyfriend at her parents' house?

Seconds later, Knox the bartender strolled in, his usual black button-down covered with a bright red vest adorned with sparkling holly berries. Over one shoulder was a Nikon camera, hanging from a strap.

Charlie rushed over to him. "You're here. Thanks for helping and for wearing the vest I gave you."

"Yeah, well, my shift doesn't start until five," he grumbled. "The vest is a lot, but it's better than a Santa hat."

Charlie turned to address Rosie. "Knox volunteered to take pictures of the kids with Santa. I'm sure their parents will be whipping out their phones, but he's a good photographer."

Knox shrugged. "It's a hobby of mine. Nothing special."

Given that Knox had a tendency to disparage himself, Rosie suspected he was downplaying his talent. "Thanks so much," she said.

"Knox is going to share the photos with us, and we can email them to the guests. I wish we had a full-on photography studio like they do at the mall, but at least these pictures will be free." Charlie tugged Knox by the elbow. "Come on. Let's get you set up."

Rosie couldn't help but smile. If anyone else but Charlie had asked Knox to help out, he would have said no. But somehow, she'd managed to convince him.

Sofia sidled over to Rosie. "Is it just me, or is that Santa kinda hot? Like, there's no way he's an old guy, right?"

"He's only twenty-seven," Rosie whispered. "When he's not playing Santa, he works as a personal trainer at the gym around the corner. We're...um...dating."

The act of admitting it still didn't come naturally, even though she and Drew had been "together" for almost a full month.

"You ever act out any naughty Santa fantasies with him?" Sofia asked. "I would love that, but I can't get my husband on board with the idea."

Why did she have to bring that up? Rosie did *not* want her mind going there, not when kids were lined up to see Santa for entirely innocent reasons.

Selena joined them and placed a hand on Rosie's shoulder.

"You okay there? Or are you staring at Drew and imagining all the titillating possibilities?"

Sofia laughed. "Hot Santas, am I right?"

Rosie wiped her forehead. All of a sudden, the close confines of the room and the thought of wicked sexual acts involving Drew were more than she could handle. "I need a few minutes to cool down. It's kind of...warm in here."

"Whatever you say." Selena grinned. "Go take a breather."

Rosie dashed out of the crowded breakfast room and headed toward the washrooms off the lobby. She raced inside, moistened a paper towel, and blotted the sweat from her forehead.

Pull it together. The Santa thing is just an act. Even if you've been dreaming about Drew constantly, those dreams aren't going to come true.

After she'd regained her composure, she left the washroom, only to run into Preston on her way back to the breakfast room. He'd swapped out his usual Brooks Brothers attire for a bright red holiday sweater and a pair of khakis.

"Rosie," he said. "Everything okay?"

"Yep. I just needed a little air. The breakfast room is at full capacity."

"Is it? That's good to hear."

But when they entered the room, she stopped cold. While families were still gathered around the different tables, working on crafts and decorating cookies, most eyes were drawn toward Santa's corner, where two kids were arguing loudly.

Shit. Why couldn't Preston have shown up ten minutes ago when all was calm?

This was *not* the impression she wanted her boss to have.

Eleven

BEFORE ROSIE COULD MAKE HER WAY TOWARD THE squabbling kids, Drew stood and straightened to his full height. When he spoke, he used his low, authoritative "Santa" voice, the one that had dominated her dreams on more than one occasion.

"Now, now," he said. "There's no need to fight. I promise I won't leave until everyone's gotten a chance to talk to me."

A girl in pigtails, probably around five or six, pointed to the boy standing beside her. "I was next in line, but he cut in front of me."

"Did not!" the boy replied. "She's lying."

"You're the liar!"

Drew knelt so he was at eye level with the girl. "Let's not worry about it, all right? I'm not sure who was first, but don't let it upset you. Spending more time waiting to chat with me means you get longer to think of what you want for Christmas." He stood and addressed the children. "Let's stay on our best behavior. That way, I can keep all of you on the nice list. Okay?"

All the children nodded, as did the parents standing next to them. Relief whooshed from Rosie's lungs as the guests resumed chatting amongst themselves. She stared at Drew in admiration, feeling more smitten than ever.

"Looks like you picked the right Santa," Preston said. "I like the way he defused the situation."

"Thank you, sir. He came highly recommended."

By the time Drew had met with all the kids in line, it was almost five, but he'd made no attempt to rush them. Only after all the families had trickled out did Rosie close up the breakfast room. Preston was long gone, and Sofia had taken off to meet with her husband. The only staff remaining were the four Damsels, Knox, and Drew, who was still dressed in his Santa outfit, minus the hat and beard.

Rosie surveyed the room critically, cringing at the cookie crumbs, the overflowing garbage can, and the bits and pieces of various crafts that littered the floor. Despite the mess, she was exceptionally pleased at what they'd accomplished.

She called everyone together. "Thanks for putting in so much work. I truly believe we gave these guests an experience they couldn't get at any other hotel in the city."

Charlie clapped her hands together. "Having the Restalls show up was a major victory. They really boosted our numbers."

"I still can't believe you got Sofia Sanchez to come here," Laurel said. "She's got a massive following."

"That was my sister's doing, but I'll pass the word along." Since Rosie would be seeing Isabella tomorrow at her parents' house for Sunday dinner, she'd thank her then. In the meantime, she planned to watch a few of her sister's "mommy influencer" videos.

"Should we get started on cleanup?" Laurel asked.

"Nope." Rosie pointed toward the door. "For now, you can all take off. I'll deal with it."

"You sure?" Charlie said. "We don't mind sticking around."

"I've got this. If anything, tidying up will help me unwind a little."

"If it's okay with you, I'd like to stay," Drew said. "Put me to work."

With a grin, Charlie grabbed Knox's arm. "Let's go. I want to try one of your new holiday cocktails."

"Can I take off this vest first?" he said.

"You look so festive in it. Please keep it on. Just for me?"

Rosie laughed when Knox agreed, albeit grudgingly. He left the room with Charlie; Selena and Laurel followed.

When Drew placed his hand on her shoulder, her skin prickled with goose bumps. "Everything okay?" she asked.

"It is, but before you start cleaning up, sit down and let me take care of you."

The affection in his voice nearly brought her to tears. When was the last time any guy had cared this much about her well-being? Certainly not her last boyfriend. Rather than offer her any way to relieve her constant, work-related tension, Erik had usually complained she wasn't being attentive enough.

"Are you sure?" she asked Drew. "You've already done so much."

"It's my pleasure. What kind of Santa would I be if I didn't spoil my best girl? Now, sit."

She did as he said, waiting as he grabbed a plate for her, piled it with snacks, and filled a cup with hot chocolate. At the first bite of a gingersnap, the sweet, spicy flavors of ginger and cinnamon flooded her taste buds. Her sister's recipe was ten times better than any store-bought version.

"Thanks," she said. "I haven't eaten since breakfast."

"I figured as much. This is just a starter. I thought I'd order some real food, too. Veggie pizza okay?"

"Sure. The only thing I don't like on pizza is pineapple."

"Oh, so you're one of *those* people. Personally, I love a good Hawaiian-style pizza."

"Weirdo. Putting fruit on your pizza is abnormal. When's the last time you heard about anyone adding watermelon to it? Or strawberries?"

He gave a rueful shake of his head. "You're the one that's missing out."

She expected him to join her at the table, but he went to stand behind her. She peeked at him over her shoulder. "Aren't you going to sit with me? You've been working as hard as I have."

"I've been sitting for over an hour. You look like you're carrying a lot of tension in your shoulders. How about a little massage?"

A massage? Rosie's face heated up, as did the rest of her body. This was a bad idea. Very, very bad.

Don't overreact. It's not sexual. It's something he's been trained to do.

"Um...okay. Let me take off my blazer." She shrugged it off and set it on the chair beside her. Under it, she'd only been wearing a sleeveless, silken shell so she wouldn't get overheated. But when Drew's hands touched her shoulders, both her pulse and her temperature spiked. Forget hot chocolate. What she needed was a big glass of ice water.

"You're so tight," he murmured as his hands kneaded her shoulders. "All that stress can't be good for you."

"It...it's not. But so much was riding on today. It's been a lot to deal with." Her voice wobbled. "I...I just can't thank you enough. For everything. Coming with me to my parents' Sunday dinners. Getting your sister to donate loads of craft supplies. Being a kick-ass Santa. All I'm doing is attending a wedding. It's hardly fair."

"You're wrong. Every time you show up at the gym and act like my girlfriend, it gives me a huge boost of confidence. Hannah and her friends love teasing me about you, and the other trainers aren't treating me like I'm a wounded puppy."

A powerful ache tugged at her heart. She was glad to be helping him. But another part of her wished it wasn't a ruse. Which was foolish because she had too much on her plate to deal with a romantic relationship. And Drew had already warned her he couldn't handle one, either.

"I'm glad I could help," she said.

As he dug in deeper, massaging stiff muscles, she let out a groan. Closing her eyes, she surrendered to the power of his hands. If he was this good at giving a massage, what was he like in the bedroom? Tender? Teasing? Did he like giving as much as receiving?

*Stop. S*he could not be thinking about sex with Drew, not when all he was doing was giving her a massage.

When he was done, he patted her on the shoulder and sat across from her. "The other thing I wanted to say? Spending time with you isn't a hardship. I enjoy it."

She gazed into his expressive brown eyes, wanting so badly to tell him everything—that she'd had a crush on him since last year, that she secretly dreamed of him at night, and that her physical desires went further than just a friendly massage.

"What is it?" he said. "You're giving me that look again."

Shit. She needed to get her emotions under control. "What look?"

He rubbed the back of his neck. "I dunno...kind of a yearning look? Like maybe you've been reading some of those Santa romances that Selena mentioned. Is it because I'm dressed in a Santa suit?"

Too flustered to deflect his question, she blurted out an honest response. "Yes. I mean...I...never had any Santa fantasies before, but now I sort of do?"

She covered her face with her hands. Why was she admitting this? Clearly, the massage had weakened her self-control.

"All Santas? Like Tim Allen from *The Santa Clause*? Or the old guy from *Elf*? Or just me?"

"Just you." The words slipped out before she could stop them.

He stared at her for a long beat. "Really? What do you fantasize about?"

"Um...sitting on your lap?" She stopped before she added the part about being naked.

"Then let's make it happen." He stood and pointed to his throne, still sitting in the corner. "Come on."

What had she done? And why was he playing along?

As if propelled by an unseen force, she followed him over to the throne. He sat on it and pulled her onto his lap. She caught a whiff of his scent, sweat mingled with a woodsy aftershave. Her heart was beating so loudly she was sure he could hear it.

He addressed her in a rumble that came from deep in his chest. "Tell me, Rosie Gonzalez. What do you want from Santa?"

She licked her lips, tasting cinnamon sugar from one of the cookies. She could have said she wanted a raise at work. A new car. A winning lottery ticket. But instead, she spoke with her heart. "I...I want you to kiss me."

His eyes widened. He pushed a stray wisp of hair behind her ear. "Are you sure about that?"

"Yes," she whispered.

"First, I want to see you with your hair down," he said.

With shaky hands, she undid the elastic and bobby pins holding her bun in place and let it cascade to her shoulders.

He cupped her face gently, smoothing his calloused palms over her cheeks. The first brush of his lips was whisper-soft, like the touch of a butterfly's wings. Wanting more, she whimpered in protest. He deepened the kiss, his tongue sweeping against hers, and she tasted hot chocolate and peppermint, which was exactly how Santa should taste. With a groan, she wrapped her arms around his neck, bringing him closer. Every inch of her body was alight, heat and desire flooding through her. For all the times she'd pined for Drew, she'd never imagined kissing him would feel this glorious.

He tangled his hands in her hair, making her whimper again as the friction sent a bolt of need straight to her core. She arched her neck, allowing him to place soft kisses on the curve of her throat. And then he was claiming her lips again, with such passion she almost forgot to breathe. She was so lost in his touch and taste that she didn't hear the door open until it was too late. She pulled away hastily, only to see Charlie standing in the doorway, holding a pizza box and a two-liter bottle of Diet Coke.

"Um...I didn't mean to interrupt, but your pizza arrived." Charlie made no attempt to hide her shit-eating grin. She set their order on one of the tables. "I'll leave you to it."

Hoping to regain a little self-control, Rosie tucked her hair behind her ears. By now, her cheeks were so warm they probably matched the red in Drew's suit.

"Thanks, Charlie," she said.

"No problem. But just FYI, the boss man's still around. He stopped by the front desk ten minutes ago to tell me a few business associates would be arriving later tonight. He wanted to make sure they got the VIP treatment."

Rosie expelled a ragged breath. Preston would never approve of her sitting on Santa's lap and making out with him like a teenager. "Thanks for the heads-up."

"Sure. Have a nice night."

After Charlie left, a wave of regret washed over Rosie. No matter how much she'd enjoyed kissing Drew, she shouldn't have done it. Not if she wanted to maintain their boundaries. "Um... maybe we should eat? Before the pizza gets cold?"

"Yeah...sorry if I got carried away."

"Don't be. I'm the one who suggested it."

He gave her a wry smile. "It was the suit, wasn't it?"

No. It was you. But she couldn't admit it. If she told him how much she desired him, she might scare him away. This whole fake-dating scheme was based on the notion they could keep things platonic.

She eased off his lap. "Definitely the suit. I blame Selena for recommending those steamy romances."

His smile vanished so quickly that she feared she'd hurt his feelings. Should she have told him how she really felt?

But then he gave a quick chuckle. "It's okay. I do make a damn good Santa. But we probably shouldn't blur the lines, not when this relationship has a definite end date."

"Right. We both have too much to deal with."

Thank God they were in agreement. This way, no one would get hurt.

So why did her heart feel like it was already breaking?

Twelve

WHILE ROSIE WENT TO GET PAPER PLATES, CUPS, AND napkins, Drew took off his Santa coat and hung it on the back of a chair. Since it was dry-clean only, he couldn't risk getting tomato sauce on it. And for both their sakes, it was time he stopped being Santa and went back to being plain old Drew.

It was the suit, wasn't it?

He'd asked it as a joke, but when Rosie confirmed it, her words were like a shot of ice water through his veins. Her bold request for a kiss had been spurred on by the fantasy of kissing a sexy Santa. Nothing more.

As he opened the pizza box, the savory smells made his mouth water. He'd ordered his favorite kind, laden with mushrooms, roasted red peppers, artichoke hearts, eggplant, and black olives. They each loaded a couple of slices onto their plates and began eating, only to lapse into a painful silence. Gone was the easy camaraderie they'd shared over the past month.

When they both reached for the soda bottle at the same time, their fingers brushed together. He pulled back as if charged by an electric current. "You first."

"Thanks." She topped up her cup and passed him the bottle.

"So…um…I just wanted to thank you for playing Santa. You did a great job, especially when you broke up that argument."

"You're welcome. Kids are pretty easy to relate to. Sometimes I help out at my sister's preschool and lead her class in fun exercises. They call me Mr. Fitness." Every time he showed up, her students greeted him like he was a rock star.

A slight smile crossed Rosie's face. "Mr. Fitness. I like it. Are you doing any more Santa appearances this weekend?"

"Nope, but next Sunday, I'm going to visit a women's shelter." He noticed a smudge of tomato sauce on her cheek and almost leaned over to wipe it off but caught himself in time. It was probably for the best if he didn't touch her right now. He passed her a napkin. "You have some sauce on the right side of your cheek."

"Thanks for catching that. I don't usually devour my food like a wild animal, but I didn't realize how hungry I was." She cleaned up the smudge. "Do you need any help next Sunday? I could come if you want, though I'm not sure what I'd wear. The only festive attire I have is an ugly Christmas sweater."

"Lucky for you, there's a matching elf costume. If you don't mind wearing it, I'd love to have you along."

Rosie laughed. "You own an elf costume? Dude, you're all-in on this holiday stuff."

To be fair, it did sound a little weird. What guy in his twenties owned a Santa suit *and* an elf costume? "I bought it last year because my sister suggested it. She thought it might be fun to help me out. She tried it a few times, but it wasn't her thing. So, I've been elf-less this year."

"Elf-less." Rosie gave a little snort. "We can't have that, can we?"

"Would you be willing to step in and be my elf? Just for next Sunday?"

"I'd be glad to."

Yes. He wanted to pump his fist in triumph. "Why don't I

drop off the costume next Saturday when I come here to play Santa? Then I can pick you up on Sunday and drive you to the shelter. Do we have dinner at your family's house that night?"

"Nope. Our next one's tomorrow—if you can make it. If not, it's okay. You've already endured two of them."

"I'm happy to do it, especially if your mom gives me more leftovers." The last time he'd brought food home, he'd made it last for two nights. There was nothing quite like coming back to his apartment after a hard day at the gym and knowing he had homemade chicken enchiladas waiting for him.

"Thanks. It's been such a relief, having you there with me. My mom hasn't nagged me about being single for a full month."

Yet another reminder that this thing between him and Rosie was an agreement. *A pact.* And if she was offering to come with him next Sunday, it was probably because she wanted their arrangement to feel more reciprocal. Which was exactly how *he* wanted it. Two good friends, helping each other get through the holidays as best they could.

When they were done eating, they pushed the tables and chairs back to their normal spots and dragged the throne and the photo booth into the storage area of the breakfast room. She retrieved a stash of cleaning supplies from a cupboard, and they got to work tidying the room.

Though they'd reverted to their comfortable friendship, every time he glanced at her, he thought about those kisses. The taste of her lips, the feel of her curves pressed against him, the little noises she'd made when he kissed her neck. A part of him wished he could have kept going. Or better yet, taken her back to his place, where he could carry out all her Santa fantasies.

Nope. Not gonna happen.

Instead, he kept his focus where it should be—on the Duchess. "Your first family Saturday went really well. You had a good crowd, and the kids enjoyed it."

"It totally exceeded my expectations, especially after the Restalls showed up."

"Do you think today's success will be enough to sway your boss? So that he'll let you keep your job?" The longer Drew spent with Rosie, the more he wanted things to work out for her.

"Probably not. We still need to increase our occupancy rate, and I'm not sure if we can make that happen between now and New Year's. No matter how many holiday amenities we offer, most people already booked their hotel stays back in the fall."

"What about reviews? I'll bet some of the families will leave five-star reviews."

She gathered up the cleaning supplies and put them back in the cupboard. "They might, but not right away. A lot of times, guests don't review a place for months, if at all. The ones who write lightning-fast reviews are usually people who are so pissed off that they can't wait to trash the hotel in a public forum."

Which was obnoxious, but not surprising. He flashed her a quick grin. "How about I make a bunch of fake accounts and leave glowing reviews? Like, 'Wow, this is the most Christmas-centric hotel ever,' or 'I love how the Duchess caters to families during the holidays!' If you need more, I'm sure my sister would write some, too."

"I appreciate the offer. Make sure you mention how top-notch our Santa was."

The twinkle in her eyes made him want to leap across the room, enfold her in his arms, and devour that sweet mouth of hers with more kisses. But he forced himself to behave.

"You and the Damsels have been working so hard," he said. "It's totally unfair that your boss could still let you go, despite all the efforts you've made."

"That's how it is in the hotel biz. If the Lyons family ever sold the Duchess to a chain—like Fairmont or Hilton—the new owners would probably bring in their own team of managers. It happens all the time." She scanned the room. "I think we're good here, so let's get going. I'll lock up behind us."

As they left the breakfast room and headed toward the lobby, Drew was pleased to note how busy it was. A bunch of the Restalls were clustered around the fireplace, talking loudly. Another group occupied the plush gray couches, their raucous laughter carrying clearly. At the front desk, the clerks wore Santa hats and were bopping around to the Jackson 5's version of "Frosty the Snowman."

The Duchess was definitely rocking a holiday vibe. But would it be enough?

Thirteen

Outside the hotel, the rain had finally let up, leaving a fine mist lingering in the air. After spending two hours in an overheated room, while wearing a Santa suit, Drew appreciated the cooler temperature. He was tempted to sprint back to the gym and change into his regular clothes, but if he left now, Rosie might take that as her cue to head home. He wanted to steal a few more minutes alone with her, so he suggested they walk for a bit.

They crossed the street and headed toward the Inner Harbour, where Victorian-style lampposts were decked out with wreaths and holiday lights that glowed in the mist. Despite the damp, chilly weather, crowds of people were out enjoying the evening. A few boats in the harbor had twinkling white lights strung along their masts, and in the distance, the city's iconic Parliament Buildings were lit up; a flourish of red and green lights adorned the dome atop the largest one. Seeing all the décor put Drew in a festive mood.

They'd just walked down to the causeway that ran along the waterfront when Rosie turned to him. "I've been meaning to ask. What happened with that fitness manager position at your gym? Did Bones find someone to take over for Jared?"

Drew responded with a touch of pride. "No one wanted the extra responsibility, so I told Bones I'd do it. We're meeting to discuss it on Monday."

"That's great." Her voice rose with excitement. "What made you decide to go for it?"

"You did. Well, partly the raise and the benefits, but you were the catalyst."

"Me?" She placed a hand over her heart. "I'm flattered, but I hope I didn't pressure you."

"You didn't. But I've spent the past month watching you engage with your team at the hotel. You don't just give them orders, but you also play on their strengths and listen to their suggestions. I've been thinking about ways we could improve the training program at Northlife, and I'd love to get all the staff on board."

When he'd told Bones he was hoping to make a few changes, his boss's positive reaction confirmed that he'd made the right decision.

"What kind of improvements?" Rosie asked.

"I'd like us to customize our sessions to better accommodate elderly clients or people recovering from injuries. I also want to make sure our trainers aren't so elitist that they'll only take on clients who are already in great shape."

"Do trainers actually pick and choose like that?"

"Yeah. Jared's one of the worst examples." Drew didn't want to rag on the guy yet again, but thinking about that selfish prick made him heat up with anger. "Hannah told me that he's made disparaging comments about her and some of her friends. Like, they're not worth training if they've got one foot in the grave."

Rosie scowled. "That's horrible. I think it's so inspiring that they're still going to the gym on a regular basis. I hope I'm half as active when I'm their age."

"Same here. He's also criticized gym members who are overweight or out of shape, which is total bullshit. Trainers like him make people hesitate to join a gym. I don't want that. Fitness is for everyone." He gave a short laugh. "Sorry if that sounded like a PSA."

"Don't apologize. Your attitude rocks. For me, joining a health club wasn't just about getting fit; it also made me feel good about myself. You always emphasized that when I worked out with you."

Her words of validation enveloped him like a warm hug. "Exactly. I want to be more thoughtful and inclusive around all our clients." He'd been formulating his ideas over the past two weeks, but only now was he able to fully articulate them. Rosie's presence had that effect on him.

"This is such a great opportunity for you," she said. "Now I *have* to stay on at the Duchess. Otherwise, I won't get to see you as much, especially if I can't find a job in Victoria."

The thought of her leaving sent shock waves through him. "I didn't think you'd have to move."

"Hopefully not, but I need to be flexible. I'd start with hotels in the Greater Victoria area, then look up island, like Nanaimo or Duncan. But I'd rather not move, not with my family and friends so close by."

On impulse, he took her hand and gave it a squeeze. "I don't want you to move, either."

Time stood still as she locked eyes with him. He yearned to take her in his arms and promise her everything would be all right. But if he held her, he'd want to do more than just give her a hug.

When she whispered his name, like a gentle caress, he reacted instinctively, brushing his fingers against her cheek. Giving a soft little sigh, she leaned toward him, her lips parted. Having her this close was too hard to resist. He no longer cared about their boundaries. All he wanted to do was kiss her again.

Before he could claim her lips, a loud whistle shattered the stillness.

"Woo! Get it, Santa!" A pack of teenage boys strolled by, laughing at the two of them.

Rosie pulled away abruptly. "I...I should probably go. It's been a long day."

Damn. "Yeah. Of course. I'll bet you're exhausted. I can walk you back to the hotel. I need to head over to the gym and change out of my Santa gear."

"Thanks. Now that my adrenaline is wearing off, I just want to go back to my apartment, change into my pajamas, and spend the rest of the night watching Christmas movies."

He wished he could join her. Hang out at her place, make popcorn, and watch *Elf* or *A Christmas Story*. But he didn't suggest it because he didn't trust himself to be alone with her right now. If she gave him even the slightest encouragement, he'd end up kissing her again.

After parting ways with her at the hotel, he went back to Northlife Fitness, changed in the locker room, and headed home. Once he got to his apartment, he called out to his roommates but didn't get a reply. No surprise since it was a Saturday night and they usually went out drinking, then ended up at a club. *No, thanks.* Drew had tried the club scene when he first moved to Victoria, but he wasn't much of a night owl, especially since some of the classes he taught started at seven in the morning.

As usual, the kitchen was a disaster, with dirty dishes piled in the sink and the trash overflowing with takeout containers from Wing's Chinese restaurant. Not for the first time, he wished he had his own place, but rent in Victoria was sky-high. He'd deal with the mess later. Right now, he needed to cool off with a beer.

He plopped down on the couch with a bottle of Labatt Blue and turned on the TV, flicking through the streaming services until he found one of his favorite '80s action flicks—the first *Terminator* movie.

For a moment, he was tempted to text Rosie and suggest they do a watch-along, but he didn't want to come across as too intrusive. Besides, she'd probably settled in with a Christmas movie by now. When his phone rang, he answered it quickly and was pleased to hear his sister's voice come on the line.

"Hey, Drew," Kate said. "How'd it go at the Duchess? I wish I could have helped instead of being stuck at Lola's bridal shower. It was *the worst*."

Uh-oh. For the past week, Kate had been looking forward to the shower. Had she hit her limit? He turned off the TV. "What happened? Too much socializing?"

"That part wasn't so bad. But Lola's obnoxious younger sister organized the shower, and she went the raunchy route. We're talking games like pin-the-junk on the hottie, dirty Pictionary, and Truth or Dare. I'd just as soon block it from my memory, so tell me about your event at the hotel. Were the crafts a big hit?"

"They were fantastic. The kids loved them." At her urging, he filled her in but didn't stop there. With some reluctance, he told her about kissing Rosie and the awkwardness that had ensued afterward.

"I screwed up," he muttered. "But now I can't stop thinking about it."

"When you told me about this pretend-dating scheme, I was all for it. Anything to show Evelyn you'd moved on. But it's not just about that anymore. Right?"

"Yeah. Rosie and I...we're friends now. I like spending time with her."

"Then why not go out with her for real? She's obviously into you. When I dropped off the craft supplies with her friend Charlie, we both agreed you need to stop with the fake shit."

"You were talking about us?" He cringed, imagining the conversation.

"It just came up. But seriously, tell Rosie you're done pretending. It's that simple."

"No, it's not," he grumbled. Usually his older sister's advice was spot-on, but not this time. "She's too busy at the hotel. And if she doesn't meet her boss's demands, she might be looking for a new job in January. Which means she could end up anywhere. She won't want to be tied down by a romantic relationship."

"That's weak, and I don't buy it," Kate said.

"I'm serious. She's dealing with a lot of stress." Over the past month, he'd seen how overwhelmed she was. Even though she claimed to love a challenge, she was being pushed to her limits.

"This isn't about her. It's about you and your fear of getting hurt. It all boils down to your trust issues."

He peeled the label off his bottle and crumpled it into a ball. "I don't have trust issues."

Which was a lie, because of course he did, after years of growing up in a family where his parents had heaped abuse on each other. And then turned on him whenever he tried to intervene.

"You totally do, and I get it. Our folks did a number on us. Every time I'm around them, I think, 'How the fuck could I ever trust anyone enough to marry them? Why put in all that effort if it's going to turn out like that?' But just because we spent years watching them tear each other down doesn't mean we're gonna end up like them." When he didn't respond right away, she drove out a harsh sigh. "Listen, bud, I know I sound like a broken record, but I think you should consider therapy. It's helped me a lot."

He didn't want to revisit this argument. The one time he'd asked his parents if they'd ever tried counseling, they'd called it a waste of money—a crutch for people too weak to solve their own problems. Even though he *knew* they were wrong, their comments had stuck with him.

"Most of the time, I get by okay," he said. "It's just hard for me to open myself up to anyone. And then, when I finally did—"

"She screwed you over royally."

"To be fair, it wasn't one-sided. She claimed I wasn't letting her in completely, and she was right."

"Yeah, but she didn't have to cheat on you with her old boyfriend and then gaslight you for weeks. She was manipulative as hell. I should know, seeing as how I dated someone just like her."

True enough. Kate's last girlfriend hadn't been much better. If anything, she'd been worse because she'd stolen money from Kate. Since then, his sister hadn't dated anyone new.

"I guess we're both kind of broken," he said.

The minute the words were out, he regretted them. He didn't want to think of himself that way. He wanted to be good old Drew Richardson, the easygoing personal trainer everyone liked. The happy-go-lucky Santa who loved making kids smile.

When Kate spoke up again, her voice was weary. "The thing is —we don't have to stay broken. We can do better, and it starts with trusting the right people. Rosie sounds like that kind of person. If I found someone like her, I'd be willing to take the risk again."

"Kate..."

"Just think about it, okay?"

"Okay. Thanks."

But even as he agreed with her, he knew he wouldn't follow through. Better to enjoy what he and Rosie could offer each other —friendship, support, and camaraderie—than try for something that would leave another scar.

He'd just have to make sure he and Rosie didn't end up in a situation where they'd be tempted to blur the lines again.

Fourteen

There were Mondays, and then there were Mondays. And this morning was a large caramel latte with two shots of espresso Monday, especially since Rosie had set her alarm two hours early so she could get to the hotel by seven. Thanks to all the time she'd invested in making the Duchess "holiday forward," she was behind on her paperwork. Unread emails sat in her inbox, demanding replies. Job applications for a new breakfast room attendant needed to be reviewed. She also had to work with Charlie to figure out staffing for the front desk because they'd lost two of their clerks.

It didn't help that she was woefully sleep-deprived. Not just because she feared losing her job but also because she was afraid she'd messed things up with Drew.

On Saturday, when he'd teased her about having sexy Santa fantasies, she could have responded by bantering with him. Kept things light and flirty, without crossing any lines. Instead, she'd asked for a kiss. An impulsive move that had resulted in a passionate make-out session she couldn't forget. Though they'd both agreed it was a bad idea, she'd almost asked him to kiss her *again* when they'd been out walking afterward.

In retrospect, it was a good thing those teens had interrupted the moment by catcalling them.

Cradling her coffee and a box of pastries—for a meeting with the Damsels at eleven—she unlocked her office door. She set everything down on her desk and turned on her computer, hoping to tackle a few of her emails. But she couldn't focus.

Instead, she remembered how she'd felt on Saturday evening, after she'd gone home to her apartment. She'd tried watching TV, but her mind kept drifting back to those kisses. What would have happened if Charlie hadn't interrupted them? Would Drew have kept going? Would he have taken things further?

Yes, please.

To compound the awkwardness, the two of them had been expected for dinner at her parents' house the very next day. Unlike the past two dinners, he'd met her there rather than driving with her. Though he'd been as outgoing as ever—regaling her family with tales of playing Santa—he hadn't spent any time alone with her. After dinner, they'd parted ways quickly.

Which meant he was probably regretting those kisses.

Her best option was to ease back into their regular friendship. A damn shame, considering how badly she wanted to kiss him again. Or do more than kiss, if she was being honest.

She turned her attention back to her emails, flagging the ones she needed to deal with first. When her phone rang and the caller ID displayed the name Alejandro, she recoiled instinctively. As the assistant general manager of the Grand Duke, he was at the same level she was, but he always treated her like she was beneath him.

Even so, she had to play nice with a fellow hotelier. Or should she say, *hospitalitarian*, which was how he referred to himself.

Gritting her teeth, she answered the phone politely. "The Duchess Hotel, Rosie Gonzalez speaking. How may I help you?"

"Rosalina. How's my favorite AGM doing?" Despite his

overbearing smugness, there was no denying his smooth Castilian accent was enticing as hell. Word had it that he was a consummate womanizer. "I saw your little hotel made the paper on Friday. It must have been *so* exciting for you."

Could you be any more condescending? "Thanks. It was a nice article."

"A little birdie—I mean, a peon from our marketing department—told me Sofia Sanchez showed up at your event. I'm not sure if that makes you look hip or desperate."

Rosie took another sip of coffee. It was too early for this shit. "Is there a reason you called? As much as I'm enjoying our chat, I've got a lot of work to do."

"Yes, well, I need a teeny favor from you, *querida*."

She perked up immediately. A favor? In what world did anyone from the Duke ever ask for a favor? "What can I do for you?"

"Long story short, last night, we had a dreadful kitchen fire in the restaurant. It was a total disaster."

Even if Rosie could barely stand Alejandro, or pretty much any of the senior staff at the Duke, she could sympathize. "That's awful. Was anyone hurt?"

"A few of the kitchen staff suffered minor burns. Then we fired the line cook who started it because he was drunk. Now we have to close the restaurant, which isn't ideal during the holiday season. To make things worse, the rooms above the kitchen suffered serious smoke and electrical damage. We were able to move the guests around temporarily, but we have a sizeable group coming this afternoon that needs their rooms. And—as you probably guessed —we're fully booked this week."

Of course you are. "Why not prioritize the existing guests and move the incoming group somewhere else?"

"No can do. They're here for a convention. Something to do with green energy? Or conservation? We can't boot them out, not if we want their group to return next year."

As the realization struck Rosie, she couldn't help but grin. "So you're asking *us* to host the displaced guests?"

Over the past year, there had been a few times when other hotels in the area had "walked" their guests to the Duchess—a hotel term that meant sending them elsewhere versus *literally* walking them over. But the Grand Duke had never sent guests their way.

"We didn't have much choice," Alejandro said. "Usually we'd ask the Hotel Grand Pacific or the Magnolia to accommodate them, but they're full. And we all know your hotel hasn't exactly been overflowing with guests."

Ignoring his dig, she responded cheerfully. "We'd be happy to help. If you want to send them over, I'll alert the staff, and we'll make sure we have rooms ready for them."

"Knew I could count on you, princesa. I'm sending you an email with all the details. Keep in mind that these guests might be a tad grumpy since the Duchess is a considerable downgrade. But I'm sure you'll do your best."

The downgrade comment was uncalled for, but she let it pass. After chatting with him for a few more minutes, she ended the call and refreshed her email. Sure enough, the list was there. Enough guests to bump their occupancy rate to a whopping eighty-five percent. Not wanting to waste any time, she radioed housekeeping and the front desk.

Minutes later, a knock came at her door. "Come in," she called out.

Charlie popped her head in. "I can't believe Alejandro is sending guests here!"

Rosie motioned her inside. "I know, right? But we have rooms available, and we're only a block away from the Duke. I'll take it as a win."

"It's a major win." Charlie clasped her hands together. "We have to make these poor souls feel like VIPs. Free drink coupons for our weeknight happy hour. Christmas cookies. Maybe a few other goodies. They're going to love it here."

"They might not be that appreciative. If anything, they'll be pissed they got booted from the Duke."

"Then we'll make this a positive experience for them. But right now, we're understaffed because Bri's home with the flu. Any chance you could jump in and help me out?"

"Absolutely. I forwarded you Alejandro's list, but let me print out a copy for myself." Rosie took another sip of coffee and winced, realizing it had gone cold. She'd have to reheat it in the microwave later.

"I'm so glad we're getting more guests," Charlie said. "I forgot to mention—we got a couple of stellar reviews on Expedia. Both were from families that were part of the Restall reunion. They loved our holiday activities."

"That was quick. Most of the Restalls just checked out yesterday."

"Laurel also told me one of Sofia's videos got tons of views! Guess which one it was."

Rosie grabbed a peppermint candy from a bowl on her desk and popped it into her mouth. "The video with the photo booth?"

"No. The one where she talked about our 'hot Santa' and showed her viewers what a delight he was."

"What?" Rosie's heart began beating frantically. This was too much excitement for a Monday morning. "What hot Santa video?"

"You didn't see it? Oh my God, it was awesome!" Charlie took out her phone and pulled up the video. "Check it out."

Rosie watched in stunned silence. At some point, Sofia had conducted a mock interview with Santa, where she teased him about his workout regimen. Drew had played along, telling her how he could lift a reindeer over his head and did weight training using sacks of toys.

How had Rosie missed it? Maybe it had happened while she was taking a breather in the washroom. Either way, there was no denying Drew was a complete charmer, his eyes twinkling as he bantered with Sofia.

She handed the phone back to Charlie. "Why does he keep getting more irresistible? How am I supposed to keep things platonic?"

"From what I saw on Saturday, you're way past that point. If I hadn't interrupted, you two might have had sex in the breakfast room."

Rosie frowned. "I'd never do anything so unhygienic. Not to mention, there are two security cameras in that room."

"I guess it's not *that* romantic. But you could have brought him back to your apartment afterward." Charlie placed her hand over her mouth. "Ooh, is that what you did?"

Rosie grabbed the guest list from the printer. "No. Kissing him was a mistake, and it's not going to happen again." She ushered Charlie from her office and locked the door behind her.

As they strode toward the front desk, Charlie lowered her voice. "Why can't it happen again? You two are so good together."

"That's not what Drew wants, and I'm not about to pressure him. One of the reasons we're pretending to date is to avoid all the stress and heartache of a real relationship."

"You sure? Because you seem stressed right now." Charlie's brow furrowed. "We're gonna put a pin in this, but we'll talk later. All of us. If I can't convince you, then maybe Selena and Laurel can."

Before Rosie could respond, they'd reached the front desk. After greeting the clerk on duty, she settled in and pulled up the day's bookings. When her phone pinged, she was pleased to see a message from Drew.

Drew: Just talked to Bones! I'm in! We're going to take care of the paperwork tomorrow.

Rosie: I'm so excited for you! I have some fun news about the hotel, too.

Drew: Are you coming to work out tonight? We could grab smoothies after and catch up.

Was this a good idea? Or should they stick to their specific "date" activities, like Sunday dinners and events at the hotel?

Screw it. Today had turned from bad to good, and she wanted to share her victory—however minor—with Drew.

Rosie: I'll be there after seven. Can't wait!

As she noticed Charlie smirking at her, she stashed her phone in the pocket of her blazer. But she couldn't stop herself from grinning like a fool. Not just about today's news but about how excited she was to share it with someone who cared.

Fifteen

AFTER FINISHING UP HER EVENING WORKOUT, ROSIE SAT with Drew at the gym's smoothie bar. As always, he looked totally mouthwatering, wearing the red fleece hoodie she loved—the one that made her want to snuggle with him. At her urging, he told her about his meeting with Bones, then asked about her news. Still glowing with excitement, she explained how the Duke's misfortunes had given them a surprise influx of new guests.

"How were they?" he asked. "Did you get a lot of complainers?"

"A few, but we did our best to win them over. Free drink coupons, cookies, and holiday goody bags. It was amazing what Charlie put together on such short notice."

"What did your boss think?"

She sipped her strawberry banana smoothie, a tasty reward after an extra-grueling workout. "He played it cool, but I could tell he was secretly gloating."

"Maybe we'll get lucky and the Duke will have another mishap. A burst pipe would do the job nicely." Drew gave an evil laugh, worthy of a cartoon villain. "We should get a crew together and cause some mayhem."

She laughed along with him. "As much as I love the idea, I don't want to spend Christmas in jail."

At the sight of Evelyn approaching them, her shoulders tightened. Over the past month, she'd run into Drew's ex occasionally, but she'd kept their interactions as brief as possible. She reached over and took his hand.

He gave it a quick squeeze before smiling up at his ex. "Hey, Evelyn. How's it going?"

Her gaze dipped down to their hands, a brief frown crossing her face before she replaced it with a neutral expression. "I'm stretched way too thin. Working here full-time and planning an extravagant wedding reception isn't for the faint of heart."

"Sorry to hear it, but I'm looking forward to your wedding," Rosie said. The minute the words were out, she regretted her simpering tone.

"I'm glad you can make it," Evelyn said. "Did Drew tell you the dress code is formal? I hope that won't be too much for you, but my parents wouldn't have it any other way."

Did Evelyn expect her to be cowed by the idea of dressing up? "No problem. I already found a killer dress, and I can't wait to wear it." She wasn't about to mention that she'd bought it on clearance.

"Glad to hear it. Good luck getting *this* one into a suit." Evelyn gestured to Drew. "He's only happy if he's wearing workout gear."

Rather than respond with a barb of his own, Drew tugged on Rosie's hand. "We should get going if we want to hit Centennial Square tonight."

Though she couldn't remember if he'd mentioned this earlier, she was happy to play along. She finished her smoothie and stood up beside him. "You bet. Let's do it."

"See you later," Drew said to Evelyn.

Only after they were outside did Rosie speak up again. "What was that about?"

He blew out a frustrated breath. "I've been doing my best to avoid Evelyn. Ever since you and I started dating, she's ramped up the passive-aggressive comments."

"She's probably resentful that you've gotten over her. That's a good thing, right?"

"It is, though I could do without the snark. I'll be glad when she and Jared are gone."

Rosie couldn't imagine working with her ex, especially after the nasty way he'd treated her during their breakup. Thankfully, Erik was a real estate broker, so there was no chance of their worlds overlapping. "Sorry you have to deal with that. Anything I can do to help?"

"Just seeing you at the gym always boosts my mood."

"I've enjoyed getting back into it. Not gonna lie, watching you flex all those muscles is a definite perk."

The minute she said it, she wanted to clamp her hand over her mouth. Why had she admitted she'd been ogling him? Friends didn't do that to each other.

But he responded with a grin. "Right back at you. And when you wear those bike shorts? The ones with the racing stripe down the side? Yes, please."

A few times, she'd suspected he might be staring at her ass. Knowing it was true made a burst of desire flare up inside of her.

Fuck. How was she supposed to keep their boundaries in place?

She looked away, taking a moment to compose herself. "So...*are* we going to Centennial Square to see the lights?"

"If you want. Sorry I dragged you out of the gym before you could grab your coat."

"It's okay." Though she wished she had her gloves and hat, her fleece pullover was plenty warm. And she didn't protest when he put his arm around her shoulder and pulled her closer.

But as they started walking, she was careful to keep her lustful thoughts to herself. Even if it killed her, she was not about to cross the line again. Which meant no bringing up Saturday's kisses or hinting at the spicy dreams they'd inspired.

Unlike the past two nights, the sky was cloudless, giving them a clear view of the quarter moon. A slight breeze blew off the ocean, but otherwise, the temperature was warm for December. As they strolled along Government Street, past the tourist shops selling gifts and souvenirs, Rosie delighted in all the holiday displays. Like the store with the giant stuffed moose in front, now wearing a Santa hat. Or the bakery whose front window was adorned with a row of intricately decorated gingerbread houses.

Given the mild weather, Rosie wasn't surprised at the abundance of couples and families gathered around Centennial Square, a large, open-air plaza located near Victoria's Chinatown. At the front of the square, a giant archway was lit up with multicolored bulbs. Dozens of trees adorned with twinkling white lights were scattered around the area, and Christmas songs played through the speakers. The central fountain was lit up, the spray of water glowing purple and red.

"This is so beautiful," she said. "Thanks for bringing me here."

"You've seen it before, right? They do this every December."

She gave a sad shake of her head. "I've always been too busy. I need to take time for more stuff like this."

"You really do. Not out of obligation, but to relax and enjoy yourself."

"Do you think I work too hard?" Even as she said it, she braced herself for the usual criticism, the kind she got from her family. That she was too driven, too single-minded, too obsessed with her career.

"That's not for me to judge. Sure, you work a lot, but you love your job. Every time you solve a problem or deal with a crisis, you get all fired up. Like you can handle anything. It's amazing."

Blinking back tears, she turned to face him. "No one's ever said that to me. Like my intensity is a good thing."

"It's awesome. You don't have to change. But if you want a break, that's okay, too. Just say the word, and I'll gladly join you."

He was so considerate. Such a good friend.

A friend. Something she should keep in mind rather than wishing they could continue where they'd left off on Saturday. That road would only lead to misunderstandings and hurt feelings.

But once she was back in her apartment, alone in bed, she couldn't stop herself from indulging in a few wicked fantasies involving Drew. And, once again, she desperately wished he was there to share them with her.

Sixteen

16 Days Until Christmas

On Sunday afternoon, Drew showed up at Rosie's apartment dressed in his Santa gear. When she greeted him at the door, he couldn't help but stare. Clad in the red-and-green elf costume he'd loaned her, she looked decidedly...sexy.

Clearly, the costume was a size too small for her curvy build—an observation he should have made much sooner. The green bodice strained against her full breasts, and the flared red skirt hugged her butt. Beneath the skirt, dark green tights accentuated her shapely thighs and calves. The only part of her outfit that wasn't lust-inspiring was her black ankle boots.

Rosie placed her hands on her hips. "I know I look like 'Santa's sexy little helper,' but this costume is obviously meant for someone smaller than I am."

"Sorry. I didn't think this through. Which is a huge fail, considering I work with people's bodies all the time." He took off his Santa hat and scraped a hand through his hair. "There's no excuse for my ignorance. You don't have to come."

"Are you saying you don't want me there? Do you know how hard it was to get this outfit on?"

"No, I'd love to have you join me. As long as you don't...um... bend over. That skirt's pretty short, and—"

"No problem. I'm covered." With a laugh, she flipped up her skirt, revealing bike shorts underneath. "I won't be flashing anyone today, I promise."

He blew out a ragged breath. If he spent any more time staring at her, he might lose all self-control. They needed to leave—now.

"Okay," he said. "Let's get going. I stashed the sack of presents in the trunk of my car."

On the drive, she switched the music to a holiday station and sang along enthusiastically. She'd been so busy this week that he was grateful to get a little time with her.

"You doing okay?" he asked. "I haven't seen you at the gym since Monday."

"I know, and I hate that," she grumbled. "I was just getting into a good workout routine. But with the holiday events and all the new guests, I've been swamped."

"Let me guess—the displaced guests from the Duke require an extra level of service?"

"Some of them have been great. But there are others who are upset that our hotel isn't up to the Duke's standards. It's a lot for the front desk to deal with, so I've been running interference."

It annoyed him that people would be so petty. And he hated the thought of anyone treating Rosie rudely. "I hope they aren't being too obnoxious."

"I can handle it. On the plus side, our numbers are looking good. But this past week, we did four happy hours. Then, yesterday, after our family event ended, I stayed until ten."

He winced, imagining how tired she must have been. "Sorry I couldn't stick around to help you clean up."

"You did more than enough, playing Santa again. And I had plenty of help. I'm glad you got to take your sister out for her birthday. How'd it go?"

"Really well. I made reservations at our favorite Italian place and got there early enough to tell them it was Kate's birthday. After dinner, the waitstaff brought her a piece of cheesecake with a candle on it and sang to her. Kind of a goofy gesture, but she appreciated it." He was glad he'd carved out time for Kate, especially since their parents had neglected to call her. "I wish you could have come with me."

"Me, too. After the Damsels helped me clean up, I spent hours in my office getting my inbox under control. And *then* Preston wanted me to come in today to deal with a bunch of other shit. I went in for a few hours this morning, but I'm glad I had an excuse to leave early."

Drew didn't want to nag her, but he couldn't hold his tongue any longer. Not when it seemed like her boss was taking advantage of her. "I know you don't mind working the extra hours, but he's asking an awful lot of you. Have you told him how exhausted you are?"

Rather than respond defensively, she sighed in resignation. "No, but I doubt it would make a difference. He knows how much I want to keep my job, so he's going to push me hard. In all fairness, he's got a lot riding on this holiday initiative. When the owners hired him, they expected results."

Even so, she shouldn't be shouldering so much of the burden. At the last family dinner Drew had attended, Rosie's parents had chastised her for spending too many hours at the hotel. Though he hadn't sided with them, he was starting to wonder if they were right. No matter how much she loved her job, she was letting it take priority over everything else, even her own self-care.

As a trainer, he'd seen what happened when clients were so fixated on their careers that they didn't make time for relaxation and physical activity. They often burned out and ended up miserable. He didn't want that to happen to Rosie.

He parked outside the entrance of a nondescript, two-story building that resembled a small apartment complex. "A quick word about this place. It's a temporary shelter for victims of domestic violence and their children. But it's unmarked and not located on any public maps. They want to keep it that way."

She nodded. "Are they okay with you showing up? No offense, but you're a guy, and a lot of them are probably running from awful husbands."

"I might be a guy, but I'm also Santa. When I called last week, the staff made sure everyone staying at the shelter would be comfortable with my visit. Just to warn you—some of these families have been through a lot. Even so, you can't cry in front of them. Our mission is to spread joy."

"I'll stay upbeat. I promise."

Upon entering the shelter, they headed for the lobby. The first time Drew had seen it, he'd been pleasantly surprised. Even if the linoleum was scuffed and the furniture was slightly worn, the walls were covered with vibrant paintings—flowers, streetscapes, and mountain scenes. Rainbow-striped rugs and potted plants added more pops of color. But as welcoming as the place appeared, the people staying here had endured a lot of hardships. Last December, during his initial visit, he'd struggled to control his emotions. Playing the role of Santa hadn't been easy when his heart was nearly breaking.

But he'd told himself if he could brighten someone's day— even for an hour or two—then it was worth the effort.

An elderly white woman, whose gray hair bore a few purple streaks, stood behind the front desk. She gave him a warm smile. "Good afternoon, Santa. You're right on time. I see you brought a helper with you."

Rosie curtsied. "Pleased to meet you. Rosie the Elf at your service."

"Aren't you a cutie? Everyone's been looking forward to this. A few of our volunteers even brought in cookies." She pointed down the hall. "Santa, I believe you know the way?"

"I do, thanks." He walked toward the shelter's community room with Rosie. As they approached it, the sound of children was unmistakable. He paused for a few seconds and gave himself a tiny pep talk.

Remember, good vibes only. You're Santa, you love kids, and you live to bring them joy.

Like the lobby, the community room was decorated with vivid paintings, colorful rugs, and potted plants. Most of the space was occupied by folding tables and chairs, along with a few shelves of books and games. Off to one side was an artificial Christmas tree decorated with lights and an assortment of homemade ornaments.

Waving at the families, Drew headed toward the tree and set his sack beside it. "Ho, ho, ho! Merry Christmas, everyone! It's so good to see all of you."

By his count, about a dozen families were scattered around the room. Most of the children were on the younger side, though one woman was accompanied by two girls who looked like middle schoolers.

"Santa!" A little girl leapt to her feet in excitement. She couldn't have been more than three, dressed in a faded Cinderella T-shirt and a plastic tiara.

"Are you bringing us presents?" another boy asked.

"That's what I live for," Drew said. "I've got something for everyone. First, I'd like you to meet Rosie the Elf. She's my assistant manager, which means she's in charge of bossing around the other elves at my workshop."

With a grin, Rosie waved at the group. "Hi, there. I was so excited when Santa invited me to join him as his helper. I'll bet you can't wait to talk to him, right?"

When the kids agreed, Drew pulled up a chair next to the Christmas tree. "Before you tell me what you want, do you have any questions? Like, about my reindeer or my elves? Or my lightning-fast sleigh that travels around the world in just one night?"

Kids loved asking questions. Even if they didn't always believe his answers, he could usually make them laugh.

"Is Rudolph really one of your reindeer?" a girl asked. "Or was he made up for that show?"

"Ah, Rudolph." Drew gave a sad shake of his head. "He's real, but the fame turned him into a total attention hog. He's all, 'Look at me and my brilliant nose,' when the other reindeer work just as hard. Personally, my favorite is Dasher. He's got the moves."

As Drew's helper, Rosie stood at his side, smiling as he fielded questions from the children. Though they ranged in age from two years old to twelve, he managed to get a laugh out of all of them. Sure, he'd probably done this dozens of times, but he didn't seem bored or jaded. After each child took their turn talking to him, he gave them a gift bag filled with simple presents, like Hot Wheels cars, coloring books, Play-Doh, stickers, and small stuffed animals.

Through it all, Rosie regarded him with admiration. At the Duchess, his jolly version of Santa had gotten rave reviews, but today, he displayed an extra level of caring. Was he making up for what he'd lacked at home? Or was it just in his nature to be so thoughtful?

Around her, the mothers were smiling, but a few looked haggard. Some held their children tightly in their arms, like they were afraid to let go. Rosie couldn't imagine being in a situation like this. She'd been lucky to grow up in a home where she'd always received plenty of love.

When Drew was done, she organized a few rounds of holiday bingo and gave out grocery store gift cards to the moms in attendance. She also tried to lead them in a sing-along, but most people only knew the words to "Frosty the Snowman" and "Rudolph the Red-Nosed Reindeer." Drew joined in loudly, seemingly unbothered that he was totally off-key.

By the time they left, the day had caught up with her. All the late nights of work, the hours behind her computer, and the emotional impact of visiting the shelter had drained her. On the drive back to her apartment, she let her head rest against the passenger-side window and closed her eyes.

"Are you all right?" Drew asked.

"Just tired. And thinking about the shelter. It's such a dismal situation. Not the place itself, which seems nice and nurturing. But the circumstances."

"I agree. It makes me grateful for what I've got. Maybe life dealt me a shitty hand when I was younger, but now I have a great job and a lot of friends in my corner. That's what matters."

I could fall in love with this guy.

The thought hit her, lightning-fast, and she tried to brush it away just as quickly. Romantic love was the last thing she needed right now. What with the demands of her job, she barely had time for herself, let alone another person. And Drew didn't want romance, either. All he needed from her was friendship and a date for his ex's wedding.

When they got to her apartment, she invited him in. "If you don't mind waiting, I can take off the elf costume and give it back to you. Unless you want me to wash it first?"

He stepped inside and took off his boots. "Don't worry about it. I can do it later since it needs to be washed on delicate and hung out to dry."

"Just as well since I'm way behind on my own laundry. Do you want anything to drink? A glass of water? A can of cider? I've got some pear cider in the fridge."

"I'm good, thanks." He glanced around her apartment. "Is this place all yours? No roommates?"

"Just me. I was able to afford it when I got promoted to assistant manager. Before that, I shared a three-bedroom apartment with a couple of friends, but one of them got married, and the other moved to Vancouver."

It wasn't much—just a one-bedroom place that was barely 700

square feet, with a galley kitchen, a tiny living room, and an even tinier balcony. But the building was located in Cook Street Village, a safe, walkable neighborhood filled with cute restaurants, pubs, and shops. She'd enhanced the small living space with a hodgepodge of vintage prints, Mexican ceramics, candles, and colorful throw blankets.

He walked over to a tall bookcase, where she'd filled one shelf with framed photographs of her family. "It's nice. I'll bet you love coming here at the end of the day."

"I do. It's my little refuge. Hang tight, and I'll be back in a sec."

She went into her bedroom and shut the door behind her. After shucking off her boots, she removed her bike shorts and the ugly green tights and set them beside the bed. But when she reached for the zipper in the back of the dress, she couldn't get it to budge. She yanked on it a little harder and...nothing. Cursing, she sat down on her bed to get more leverage. Still stuck. She was tempted to pull harder but didn't want to rip the fabric and ruin the costume. Giving a grunt of frustration, she stood and opened the door to her room.

"Drew? Can you help me with the zipper?"

"Sure." He walked over to the doorway. By now, he'd taken off his hat and beard but was still wearing the Santa suit.

She turned around so her back was to him. "Can you undo it? I think it got caught on the fabric."

Standing beside her, his warmth was palpable. As he reached for the zipper, his hand brushed the back of her neck, making her shiver. His touch felt so good that she wished he'd take his sweet time, but he freed the zipper easily. He tugged on it again, only to have it snag halfway down her back.

"It's still stuck," he muttered. "Hold still, and I'll try to unzip you without wrecking the whole costume."

Other than her bra, she wasn't wearing anything under the bodice, which meant her bare back was exposed to him. She sucked in her breath, quivering as his fingers grazed her skin. A flare of need flooded her entire body. She wanted him to keep touching her but without the confining costume in the way.

He pulled down the zipper until it landed above the waistline of her panties. "I think you're good, but I'll let you finish changing. I don't want to do something we'll both regret."

She swallowed, her mouth dry. Turning to face him, she inched the costume past her hips until it pooled at her bare feet. "What if I *won't* regret it?"

Seventeen

Rosie knew she'd gone too far. She was alone with Drew in her bedroom, clad only in a lacy red bra and panties, an elf costume at her feet. And he was still dressed as Santa. She felt like she was acting out a scene from one of Selena's steamy holiday romances.

He gave a short laugh. "Is this because I'm wearing the suit? Maybe it's time you switched to another set of fantasies."

If she wanted, she could brush off her comment or treat it like a joke. But she'd spent all week thinking about last Saturday's kisses and aching for Drew's touch. One time couldn't hurt, could it?

She stepped out of the costume and pressed her hands against his chest. "This isn't about the suit. True, you're the hottest Santa I've ever seen, but I don't want Santa. I want you, Drew Richardson."

She was trembling all over, afraid he'd turn her down. If asking for a kiss was bending the rules, then begging for more was breaking them completely.

"I want you, too," he murmured. "But this isn't part of the deal."

"It could be, right? Since we're already friends, why can't we be friends with benefits? At least until the holidays end?"

Seriously, Rosie? What makes you think you can do this and not get hurt?

She'd never been the type to indulge in casual hookups or one-night stands. For her, giving someone her body usually meant giving them her heart as well. But Drew was right here, and she'd wanted him for weeks. Based on the passion he'd shown her last weekend, she suspected he felt the same way.

"We've both been under so much stress," she said. "Wouldn't it be nice to shut out the world and blow off a little steam?"

"Hell, yes. But I don't want to hurt you, especially since I can't offer you anything more."

She toyed with the buttons of his Santa coat. "I know. I'm not asking for more."

Was she shortchanging herself?

No. This would benefit them both. Even if she'd felt a surge of love for him at the shelter, she could lock up those feelings tight. She just wanted to indulge in a little physical pleasure. Surely, she could make that happen without losing her heart to him.

He smoothed his hand against her cheek. "You're worth so much more than a fling. You know that, right?"

"I do, but right now, this is all I need." Her breath hitched, but she kept going. "If you'd rather not, I'll let it go, and we can move on."

He gave her a wicked grin. "If I'd rather not? Rosie, I've been dreaming about this for weeks." He took her hand and led her over to the flowered armchair that occupied one corner of her bedroom. As he sat down on it, he pulled her onto his lap, just like he had last Saturday. "Now, why don't you tell Santa what you *really* want?"

She settled herself against him, her whole body ablaze with longing. Dressed only in her bra and panties, she felt vulnerable and sexy at the same time. Her nipples hardened into tight peaks, demanding his attention. "It's not about the suit, remember?"

"Maybe not, but I'm going to take full advantage." He lowered his voice to the sexy growl she loved. "Don't make me ask again, Rosie Gonzalez. Tell Santa what you want."

This time, she didn't hesitate. "I want you to kiss me. Then I want you to take me to bed."

"That's a lot to ask from Santa. What are you offering in return?"

"Anything you want." She kept her voice soft and sultry. "After all, I'm your very best helper elf, here to serve you."

When he leaned down to kiss her, there was nothing tentative about it. His mouth plundered hers with a rough, demanding kiss that shook her to her very core. If she'd had any doubts that he wanted her, they were gone now. Wrapping her arms around his neck, she pulled him closer and kissed him back with equal ferocity. She nipped at his lip, tasting peppermint on his tongue, barely stopping to breathe. His hard length pressed into her, and she rubbed against him until he groaned loudly.

She wanted all of him. Every inch. Every sensation. Everything. She wanted him deep inside her, pounding into her until she cried out with pleasure. Now that she'd unleashed this part of herself, she didn't want to hold back.

Feeling bolder, she undid her bra and tossed it aside. Her panties followed soon after. The fur trim of his Santa suit felt so sensual against her bare skin.

She looked up at him, no longer afraid to reveal her deepest desires. "Ever since you showed up at my meeting dressed like Santa, I've been envisioning this scenario. Me, sitting on your lap, wearing absolutely nothing."

With a chuckle, he ran his hand along her bare arm. "Good thing I had no idea, or I would have had a hard-on every time I wore this suit."

The lust in his eyes was intoxicating. If she parted her legs for him, she had no doubt he'd willingly touch her until she came apart in his arms and shattered into a million pieces. But first, she wanted to drive him over the edge. She eased off his lap and knelt at his feet, then tugged on his pants. "Why don't you take these off, and then I can show you what a good little elf I am?"

Was it weird to be referring to herself this way? Maybe, but she was caught up in the thrill of role-playing.

"Rosie, you don't have to," he said.

"Oh, but I want to. Very much."

She tugged on his pants until he pulled them down around his ankles. His boxers followed. She inched closer, inhaling his scent before stroking him gently and teasing him with her tongue. His hands twisted her hair with just enough friction to send tingles of desire racing through her. After tormenting him a little longer, she took him into her mouth, enjoying the way he gasped in response. She could hardly believe she was bringing one of her favorite dreams to life.

DREW HAD DIED AND GONE TO HEAVEN. HOW ELSE TO explain his good fortune?

For all the fantasies he'd had about Rosie, he'd never imagined getting to experience this one. The object of his dreams, kneeling naked at his feet, going down on him while he was still dressed like Santa. He released a guttural groan as she took him deeper. Tangling her thick, silken hair between his fingers, he tugged harder until she responded with a noise that was a cross between a moan and a whimper. Fuck, that was hot. Even hotter was the sensation of watching her beneath him, her eager mouth bringing him almost to the brink of ecstasy. He couldn't wait to bury his head between her legs and return the favor.

Just as he was close to exploding, he let go of her hair. "Rosie, stop. Please."

She released him and looked up at him with those big, dark eyes. "You can keep going. I don't mind."

A tempting offer, but he wanted *all* of her. "Let me finish inside of you. Please. That way, I can feel your body next to mine."

She gave him a cheeky grin. "How can I possibly say no to that?"

As she stood to face him, she wobbled slightly, then grabbed the arm of the chair. With her dark hair falling loose around her face, her flushed cheeks, and her gorgeous curves completely exposed, she'd never looked more radiant.

She regarded him with a shy smile. "You're staring."

"I can't help it. You're so beautiful." A rush of emotion coursed through him. This wasn't just a casual hookup. With Rosie, it *meant* something.

"Thanks. But now it's your turn, Santa. Time to ditch the rest of your garb."

"I'd love to." His pants and boxers were at his feet, so he kicked them off and stood to face her. "Want to help me with the coat?"

She undid the buttons and slid it off his shoulders before pulling his undershirt over his head. Once they were both naked, he took her in his arms. Before they went any further, he needed to make sure this was what she truly wanted.

She leaned against him, resting her head on his shoulder. "Drew? Are you having second thoughts?"

He caught a whiff of her coconut shampoo as he stroked her hair. "Not unless you are. But I only want this if you're fully on board."

"I am. One hundred percent. Come on." Taking his hand, she led him over to her bed. After flinging back the covers, she rummaged in her nightstand and brought out a couple of condoms. "These should do for now. If we need more, there's some in the bathroom."

"Perfect." He lowered her onto the bed so that her head was

nestled against the pillows. "Just lie back and relax, okay? You know how much I love taking care of you."

She gazed up at him with complete trust in her eyes. "Yes, please. I give you my full consent."

He took a few seconds to enjoy the sight of her lying beneath him in all her naked glory. He wanted to touch and kiss her everywhere, but he started with her breasts, cupping them with his hands, tweaking her nipples, then sucking on them until she writhed beneath him. He could have spent hours like this, tasting and teasing, but by now, she had to be craving release. He wanted to give that to her.

When he dipped his fingers between her thighs, she was wet and slick and ready for him. He stroked her in slow circles, building up the pressure until she was twisting the sheet in her fists and begging him to keep going. He parted her legs, tasting her sweetness with his tongue, long licks that had her crying out his name. She gripped his hair and bucked beneath him, her entire body shaking as he took her over the edge. Hearing her moan in ecstasy filled him with a swell of pride. When her cries faded to soft whimpers, he trailed kisses up her stomach until he was at eye level with her again.

"That felt so good," she murmured. "All those months, when I dreamed about you, I had no idea how incredible it would feel in real life."

"Months?" They'd only been together for five weeks. "What do you mean?"

"I...oops...never mind."

"Rosie." He used his stern Santa voice. "When did you start dreaming about me?"

"Um...last year, after we first started working out together? I developed this gigantic, embarrassing crush on you."

"Last year?" Though she'd occupied his thoughts constantly, he could hardly believe she'd wanted him just as badly.

"I didn't say anything because I thought it would make things awkward." She gnawed on her lip, giving him an adorably sheepish look. "Sorry about that."

Though he was tempted to tease her, he didn't want her to think her attraction was one-sided. "Want to know a secret? I felt the same way. In fact, I almost asked you to switch trainers because I don't believe in hitting on my clients."

"You wanted me, too?" She started laughing. "I never caught on—not once."

Just knowing they'd shared the same feelings made tonight even more significant. Like they were meant to end up together.

She gave him a goofy grin. "Are we completely clueless or what?"

"We'll have to make up for lost time." He reached over to the nightstand and grabbed a condom. "Okay if I use this?"

When she nodded, he tore open the foil and put it on. He nudged her legs open a little wider and slid into her, groaning at how satisfying it felt.

She buried her face in his neck. "Yes, Drew. I've waited so long for this."

He moved slowly at first, not wanting to rush her. The sensation was incredible. Her bare skin pressed against his, the alluring scent of her sex, the way their bodies lined up so perfectly, as if they were made for each other. Even better were the little noises she made. Gasps and moans and cries of, "Yes, right there." He loved that she wasn't afraid to express herself.

When she dug in her nails, he gripped her butt harder and increased his pace. But as much as he wanted to drive in deeper, he didn't want to hurt her. "Does that feel okay?"

"Yes, but I want it even harder." She laughed. "Not like caveman-wild, since this is a cheap bed from IKEA, but don't be afraid to let go."

"Fuck, yes." His breath came in gasps as he thrust into her with more force, and she wrapped her legs around him.

"I'm coming," she cried out. "Don't stop. Please don't stop."

"I've got you." He kept going until she gave a loud wail, and her entire body clenched tight around his. Then the pleasure crested over him in waves, so intense that he was still shuddering when he collapsed on top of her. He couldn't remember the last time sex had felt this unbelievably satisfying. Not just physically but emotionally as well.

"Oh, Drew." She let out a blissful sigh. "That was amazing. All the week's tension, now magically gone. You're a miracle worker."

He kissed her forehead. "Glad to be of service."

Before getting too comfortable, he eased off her, removed the condom, and wrapped it in a tissue. He tossed it into the wastebasket and then settled back in bed beside her.

Pulling the covers around them, she nestled against him. "Can you stay for a while?"

"I'd love to. There's nowhere else I'd rather be."

As he held her, a pang of yearning shot through him. He wished this fake-dating, friends-with-benefits setup could turn into something real. A relationship where he could trust her enough to give her his whole heart and know she'd treat it with love and respect.

But he couldn't quite take that leap.

Eighteen

ROSIE AWOKE TO A DARKENED ROOM. SHE RUBBED HER eyes and took a minute to get her bearings. As her hand brushed against Drew's broad chest (his broad, *naked* chest), the world snapped into focus. Though she rarely indulged in naps, she'd somehow drifted off to sleep in his arms. No surprise since she'd been so relaxed, curled up beside the man she loved.

Correction. The man she *liked*.

This wasn't love. It was friendship combined with great sex.

If she were being completely honest, she could envision falling in love with him. But that wasn't what he wanted. And she couldn't risk asking for more. Instead, she'd enjoy every minute of their time together. No sense in dwelling on their end date when it was still four weeks away.

When Drew stirred, she ran her hand along his sturdy bicep, marveling at the feel of his muscles under her fingers. Now that their boundaries were no longer an issue, she wanted to touch him everywhere.

"Good morning," she said. "Or rather, good evening."

"Hey, there." His lips grazed the top of her head. "I didn't mean to fall asleep. I was just so comfortable."

She loved that he'd relaxed enough to let himself go. "It's okay. I crashed out, too."

"So...do we need to talk about this?"

From the hesitancy in his tone, she sensed he'd rather not, which was fine with her. "I don't think so. Our agreement hasn't changed. We're still pretending to date and still friends. Except now with added benefits."

"Like an upgrade? First class instead of economy?" He gave her butt a gentle squeeze.

His touch flooded her with desire. She smoothed her fingers over the smattering of soft brown hair that covered his chest. "First class elite. Speaking of which, I'm hoping these benefits aren't a onetime thing. I'd like to do this again."

Was she being too bold? From the gleam in his eyes, she didn't think so.

"By again, do you mean tonight? Or until our agreement ends in January?" He grinned. "If it were up to me, I'd pick the second option. One more time isn't going to be enough."

A thrill of anticipation raced through her. "Me, too. Even if I'm slammed at the hotel, I can still work in time for sex."

"Then you'd better pencil me in on your calendar. How about in your office? We could lock the door and sweep all the paperwork off your desk like they do in the movies." He spoke in a husky voice. "Wouldn't you love getting railed over your desk?"

Yes, please.

She could only imagine how hot that would be. Him flipping up her skirt and taking her from behind while she gripped the desk and moaned in abandon. Sadly, it wasn't an option.

"As much as I'd love to follow through on that, there's a security camera in that room," she said. "And my paperwork is meticulously organized."

"We'll just have to settle for the bed. Are you ready for another round, or would you rather get something to eat first? You must be starving."

Now that he'd mentioned it, she was famished. "We could order takeout, but...I should find some clothes for you. I'm assuming you don't want to put your Santa suit back on."

"I've got a gym bag in my car with extra workout gear. I can go grab it, but I'll need a robe or something."

She snickered at the thought of him trying to sneak out of her apartment, still naked. Her neighbors probably wouldn't approve. She pointed to a hook on her door, where she'd hung a plaid bathrobe. "You can use that if you want. But first...I might need that second round."

"Such a greedy little elf," he murmured, taking her in his arms.

Oh, yes. She could definitely get used to this.

On Monday morning, Rosie arrived at work feeling better rested than she'd been in weeks. Last night, after she and Drew had made love again, they'd ordered Thai food and watched TV. They'd settled on a reality show where families took holiday decorating to a whole new level. Then Drew spent the night. Cocooned in his arms, she'd pushed all thoughts of the Duchess from her mind and drifted off without a care.

When her alarm clock had gone off at six thirty this morning, she hadn't been tempted to hurl it against the wall. Instead, she'd followed Drew into the shower and joined him for a steamy romp before taking off for work.

As he left her apartment, he was whistling, looking as cocky as she'd ever seen him. *She'd* made him feel that way.

She unlocked the door to her office and set her jacket and purse inside. Rather than fire up her computer and tackle her inbox, she took her coffee (a caramel latte from Alma's) and walked over to the breakfast room.

She tried to do this once a week—sit at a table, sip her coffee, and observe the hotel's guests. Sometimes, she'd introduce herself, chat with them, and ask if they had any issues. Other times—like today—she'd tuck her name badge in her pocket and observe anonymously.

For the first time in months, the room was almost at capacity, filled with people loading their plates at the free breakfast buffet. As far as buffets went, it easily surpassed the typical continental breakfast at a chain hotel since it included hot items like eggs, two kinds of quiche, breakfast potatoes, bacon, waffles, and oatmeal, as well as fresh fruit and a decent range of pastries. The banana pecan muffins were delicious, as was the lemon poppyseed loaf.

She let her thoughts drift, remembering each detail of her night with Drew. How it had felt to fall asleep beside him. To wake up together and cuddle for a few minutes more. To chat with him in the kitchen this morning, discussing their day as if they were a married couple.

It would be far too easy to envision a life like this, but she couldn't delude herself. No matter how blissful she felt right now, it wouldn't last past January.

"Rosie?"

Preston's voice startled her out of her reverie. He stood over her table, impeccably dressed in one of his Brooks Brothers suits and a dark green tie. Unlike her, he was wearing his name badge.

"Good morning, sir," she said.

"What are you doing here?" He sat down across from her.

"Just getting a feel for our guests." She gestured to the tables around them. "This is the busiest I've seen the breakfast room in months."

"That's a good thing. Smart move keeping your badge hidden." He cast a glance toward a far table. "A few of our transfers from the Duke accosted me and wanted to know why we don't have a made-to-order omelet bar."

Rosie resisted the urge to roll her eyes since it wasn't

professional. "Those omelets cost fifteen dollars. Our breakfast is free, and it's good. Have you ever tried our banana pecan muffins? They're better than the ones at Tim Hortons."

He shook his head. "I try to avoid carbs when I can."

Your loss. "All I'm saying is that a free breakfast buffet is an amenity that isn't offered by most of the hotels in the downtown area." Now that she'd brought up muffins, she was craving one, but her boss might not approve of her snitching from the buffet. "Is there something you wanted to talk to me about?"

"I just wanted to check in since Christmas is two weeks from tomorrow. How are things going with your team? Do you feel like you're succeeding?"

"We're giving it our all. So far, we've done two family Saturday events, and they've been well attended. The weekday happy hours have drawn in a decent crowd, including guests from outside the hotel. Knox's holiday cocktails have been very popular."

He nodded but didn't display the enthusiasm she'd hoped. "What else do you have planned?"

"In four days, we're doing our first 'Festive Friday' with a hot cocoa bar, treats, and caroling. Charlie's going to accompany the guests on the keyboard, and we found someone to play guitar."

Once again, Drew's sister was coming to their rescue. As a preschool teacher, she was used to leading sing-alongs, and she knew a ton of Christmas songs.

"Good. If it goes over well, you can repeat it again next Friday."

How about a little thank-you?

Sensing none was forthcoming, she continued. "As an added benefit, when guests check in to the hotel, they now receive welcome packets that include drink coupons for our weekday happy hours, as well as coupons for half-price holiday beverages at Alma's Beanery, which is just down the street. We also worked out a deal with Island Food Tours, where our guests can get twenty percent off their basic, two-hour walking tour. And Laurel collaborated with the tourist shops on Government Street to create a coupon book for guests doing last-minute shopping."

Rather than acknowledge their efforts, he took out his phone and swiped the screen. "Speaking of shopping, I had another idea. I'd like us to go hard on Boxing Day."

It took every inch of her willpower not to let loose with a string of curses. She and the other managers had secretly hoped they'd get a reprieve between Christmas and New Year's.

"I don't know if shoppers place as much attention on December twenty-sixth anymore," she said. "I think it's more like Boxing Week now."

"Even better. I want us to offer a Boxing Week special."

"Like a discounted rate?"

That wouldn't be too hard to manage. Laurel would have to work with her marketing team to update the website, send out a round of emails, and put out some social media blasts, but it was totally doable.

"Not just that. We need to offer more incentives. Like, an early-bird breakfast—starting at six instead of seven—for shoppers. Discount coupons for stores at the Bay Centre mall. Anything else you can think of."

Seriously? This was something they should have been planning months ago, not on December tenth. She tried to keep her smile in place. "That sounds great, but we don't want to get overbooked. We're projecting a ninety percent occupancy rate over the next two weeks."

Part of their success was due to the Grand Duke's misfortune, but the Duchess had also received more bookings after word had spread about their first family Saturday.

"I'd like to see it at one hundred percent, if possible," Preston said. "When I managed the Devonshire, that's the goal I set for myself. And did I succeed? Absolutely. You just need to get in the right mindset and make it your highest priority."

Rosie couldn't hide her dismay. In all the years she'd worked at the Duchess, that feat had never been accomplished. "We'll do our best, sir."

Even as she said it, she could envision the extra work a Boxing Week blitz would entail. Just the thought of it was exhausting.

"Excellent. I'll be out of town over the next few days, so I expect you to run the ship."

"Of course." She gnawed on her lip, not wanting to appear too demanding but tired of feeling like the world's biggest doormat. "Before you go, do you know when you'll decide whether you'll be keeping me on? Not just me, but all the senior staff? It would be nice to have some reassurance."

When he frowned, her heart sank. She'd pushed him too hard. Then again, she'd been busting her ass for weeks without knowing if she'd still be employed in January.

"It's a little too soon to tell, isn't it?" he said. "I'll have to wait until we get December's final numbers. Then I can give you an answer."

Feeling firmly chastised, she fixed her bright smile in place. "I understand. Thank you, sir. Have a good trip. I'll keep this ship afloat."

"Of course you will." He gave her a quick nod, then stood and left the breakfast room.

She couldn't help but remember her discussion with Drew on Sunday. He'd thought Preston was taking advantage of her, and she was inclined to agree. Even so, she didn't have any recourse.

True, she could look for another job in hotel management, but she didn't want to leave the Duchess. She wanted to keep working with the Damsels, keep her coveted position as assistant general manager, and keep doing her best to make her beloved hotel shine.

Besides, if she worked for one of the larger chains, she'd probably start at a lower level of management. She might even get sent to one of their other properties, like a hotel in Edmonton or Toronto. She'd seen it happen to the hoteliers she'd met at hospitality conventions. That wasn't what she wanted.

For now, all she could do was keep plugging away and pray the Duke didn't finish repairing their damaged rooms until January. Otherwise, the Duchess didn't have a hope in hell of reaching full capacity.

Nineteen

12 Days Until Christmas

Having formally accepted Bones' offer, Drew was eager to take over the role of fitness manager in January. Good thing since Jared was completely focused on his wedding and upcoming move to Nanaimo. While the wedding was a popular topic among the trainers at the gym, Drew no longer flinched every time someone mentioned it. Instead, he was looking forward to showing up at the event with Rosie, enjoying her company, and taking her to bed at the end of the night.

In the four days that had passed since he and Rosie had indulged in their Santa-elf role-play, they'd squeezed in two more dates, which consisted of hanging out at her place after work, sharing dinner, and having sex. While he would have preferred to treat her to a night out, her overloaded schedule didn't allow for it. Plus, she was usually exhausted by the time she came home from the Duchess. She was now clocking so many hours at the hotel that Drew wished she would set firmer boundaries. But she was dealing with enough emotional strain that she didn't need him nagging her.

Besides, he had no right to tell her how to live her life. Not when their arrangement would be ending next month.

And yet...last night, when he'd held her in his arms, he'd started thinking about the future. The more time he spent with her, the more he could imagine taking the next step. Embarking on a *real* relationship, with all the highs and lows it entailed.

But then he remembered how Evelyn had upended his world. How the passion they'd shared had gone cold, only to be replaced by indifference and outright hostility. How her constant criticism had brought back memories of his teenage years, when he'd been at the mercy of his parents' toxic behavior. He didn't want to experience that pain again.

For that reason, it was best to keep things with Rosie as they were.

After leading an intense boot camp session at the gym, he needed to cool down before his next client. He grabbed his fleece jacket and told the receptionist he was going for a walk.

Outside, the air was brisk, the breeze off the ocean whipping at his ears. He paused at the crosswalk, waiting until a red double-decker bus loaded with tourists drove by. Given the chilly weather, he couldn't believe how many people were out sightseeing. After crossing the street, he put on his hood to block out the wind and walked down to the causeway beside the harbor.

Though he normally got his coffee from Alma's, he ducked into the nearby Starbucks. Since no one was waiting in line, he ordered a coffee for himself, then decided to grab a latte for Rosie. Even if she was too busy to chat, he could drop it off with her. The thought of seeing her immediately brightened his day.

He hustled over to the Duchess and went inside, once again appreciating how festive it looked. But he paused at the sight of a tall, slim, unnaturally tanned woman who was haranguing the front desk clerk.

"I can't believe I have to put up with this," she said. "I made my reservation at the Grand Duke weeks ago. There's no excuse for sending me to this shit heap."

"I'm so sorry," the young female clerk said. "But the Grand Duke is overbooked due to some unexpected maintenance issues."

The woman leaned on the counter, getting right up in the clerk's face. "What about the other upscale hotels around here? Like the Magnolia or the Coast?"

"They're also full. But we offer—"

"I don't care what you offer," the woman snapped. "I need to speak to the manager. *Immediately.*"

"Of course. I understand. I'll call our assistant manager right now."

Drew wanted to tell the woman to chill out, but it wasn't his place. He edged over to the lobby, stood behind the fully decorated Christmas tree, and waited to see what would happen. A minute later, Rosie strode out to the front desk, looking sharp in her navy blue blazer and matching pencil skirt. Though she was sexy as hell in workout clothes, the sight of her in business attire really turned him on.

Rosie faced the woman calmly. "May I help you?"

"Only if you can get me back into the Grand Duke. This place is a huge step down. If this isn't rectified, I guarantee you'll be getting a scathing review."

Drew still couldn't figure out why disgruntled guests always took out their animosity on the Duchess when the Duke was the one who'd given them the shaft.

Rosie flashed the woman her brightest smile. "I wish I could send you back there, I really do, but we'll try to make your stay here as pleasant as possible. Right now, we're offering a host of holiday amenities, including a wonderful weeknight happy hour, a delicious, holiday-themed free breakfast, a goody bag filled with holiday treats, and some great discounts on our local restaurants and shops."

"Do I look like I give a shit about discounts?" the woman demanded. "This place is sub-par. What kind of a dump doesn't even have a workout room?"

"I apologize for that, but we do have an agreement with Northlife Fitness, just around the corner. It's the premier health club in downtown Victoria."

Sensing a role he could play, Drew emerged from his hiding place and headed for the front desk. He couldn't miss the way Rosie's eyes lit up when she saw him, but he kept his focus on the irate guest.

"Good morning," he said, channeling as much enthusiasm as he could muster. "I just stopped by to chat with the manager, but I'm glad to be of service. I'm one of the personal trainers at Northlife Fitness, and we pride ourselves on having a top-notch facility. As a guest of the hotel, you'll be able to work out there or attend any of our classes for free."

Damn, he sounded like a freaking infomercial.

"What kind of classes?" the woman asked.

"All kinds—Pilates, yoga, spinning, you name it. Personally, I'm in charge of our boot camp classes, and most of our attendees agree that it's a challenging workout."

She raked her gaze over him, lingering on his body in a way that made him uncomfortable. But he kept his smile in place. Finally, she shrugged. "I suppose it's better than nothing. But if a room becomes available at the Grand Duke, I want to be transferred over there immediately."

"If that happens, I'll contact you right away," Rosie said. "In the meantime, Bri will get you all checked in."

As the woman turned her attention back to the clerk, Rosie inched over to Drew. Taking his arm, she led him away from the front desk and flashed him a grin. "Thank you. Great save, Mr. Fitness."

He wanted to take her in his arms and kiss her thoroughly. But since they were in a public place, he played it cool by pretending to doff an imaginary cowboy hat. "Glad to be of service, ma'am."

She glanced at the to-go cups in his hand. "Is one of those for me?"

He was tempted to tease her, but she was gazing at the cups with such longing that he didn't have the heart. "It is. I got you a vanilla latte."

She took it from him. "Thanks. I really appreciate it since today's been kind of rough. This is the third guest in a row who's complained to the front desk about the Duke situation."

"Sorry you have to put up with that."

"It's okay, but I'm also bummed because Preston just informed me that he wants to add an event on Sunday night. That means we might have to miss my family's Sunday dinner. My mom's not going to be happy about that."

Drew longed to tell her demanding boss to take a flying leap, but he didn't want to add to her stress. "Maybe you could tell your mom that you'll make it up to her after the holidays. She knows you're under a lot of pressure right now."

"I can try." Rosie took a sip of her latte. "Mmmm. So good. I'd love to stay and chat, but I have a Zoom call in a few minutes."

"No problem. I've got to get back to Northlife before my next client shows up at eleven." He gave her arm a quick squeeze.

Once he was back outside, he shivered, wishing he'd brought his gloves. The bracing wind was a harsh contrast to the warmth of the hotel's lobby. But he was glad he'd taken the time to walk over to the Duchess. Seeing Rosie—even for a few minutes—had already made his day so much better.

As he was heading back to the gym, his phone rang. He answered it without checking the caller ID, only to recoil as his mother's brittle voice came on the line.

"Drew. You didn't return my last call."

No pleasantries, no asking after his health. She always got right to the point.

He forced himself to respond graciously. Going on the defensive would just rile her up. "Hey, Mom, it's good to hear from you. Sorry I couldn't answer the phone earlier, but I was teaching a class. I was going to call you back." *Eventually.*

"Were you? Sometimes I think you deliberately avoid my calls. That's no way to treat your mother."

"Sorry, Mom." He paused at the railing overlooking the harbor. Above him, seagulls glided along the air currents. He wished he could be up there with them rather than stuck trying to placate his mother. "How are you doing?"

"I was calling to talk to you about Christmas."

Fuck. For the past two years, he'd managed to avoid going home for the holidays, mostly because his parents hadn't acted as though they wanted him there. But if his mom was extending an invitation, he'd feel guilty turning her down.

"I've got plans for Christmas Eve, but if you want, Kate and I could drive up on Christmas morning." He cringed inwardly, knowing his sister would be pissed that he'd included her. At least the drive to Cowichan Bay was less than an hour. If they played it right, they could be in and out by noon and go for brunch after.

"You're welcome to drop by, provided you can somehow pull ten grand out of your ass," his mother said. "If not, don't bother showing up because there's nothing to celebrate."

Ten grand? What the fuck? "What do you need the money for?"

"We need a new car. Or, rather, a used one. I found a guy offering a Ford Fiesta for nine thousand five. It's at least ten years old, but the mileage is decent."

Drew almost didn't want to ask. "What happened to your car?"

"Your dad totaled it. He claims he was trying to avoid a deer, but I smelled the booze on his breath. Fucking idiot. He's lucky he didn't end up in jail."

A sick feeling lodged in the pit of Drew's stomach. Though he wouldn't call his dad an alcoholic, the old man often put away four or five beers in a sitting. "Has he been drinking a lot?"

"No more than usual. But he spends most nights at that dive bar with his buddies. I'd like to burn that shithole to the ground."

I'll bet you would. Despite his frustration, Drew tried his best to come across as sympathetic. "Sorry, but I don't have any extra cash right now."

"Didn't you say you were getting a promotion? Aren't they paying you more?" When he didn't answer, her voice rose in anger. "Most kids would be glad to help their parents. You and Kate are so fucking ungrateful."

As always, the guilt hit him hard. But this time, he wouldn't give in. His parents still hadn't paid back the money he'd loaned them three years ago. "I'm sorry, Mom. But Kate and I could still come for Christmas. We'd love to see you."

"Would you? The last time you showed up for the holidays, you didn't even spend a full day with us."

"Because you and Dad started fighting. If you could lay off, just for once, I'd stay a little longer."

She let out a snort of disgust. "Don't tell me how to live my life. And if you can't pitch in and help us out financially, then you're not welcome at home." With that, she ended the call.

Emotion clogged his throat. He stood still, letting the pain wash over him, like a wave breaking on the shore.

None of this is your fault.

In his heart, he knew he wasn't to blame for his parents' misery or their financial situation, but whenever he spoke with his mom, his insecurities came racing back. His parents were proof that even the most loving relationship could turn ugly and hateful.

Rather than sink into a pit of bad memories, he forced himself to focus on the positive aspects of his life. Thanks to Rosie's encouragement, he was excited to start his new job. Spending time with her always lifted his spirits, and he'd truly enjoyed those Sunday dinners with her family. The last time he'd visited, he'd shared stories of his exploits as a volunteer Santa. Even if he'd only met her family a few times, they'd treated him like he belonged.

Thinking of them put an idea in his head. If Rosie's schedule was so overloaded that she couldn't make it to their next dinner, maybe he could arrange a way for her to spend time with them.

Twenty

11 Days Until Christmas

Rosie was running on fumes. Instead of indulging in happy hour at Pepe's, she and the Damsels were preparing the breakfast room for their first "Festive Friday" event. They'd set up a hot cocoa bar with plenty of toppings: whipped cream, sprinkles, caramel sauce, crushed Oreos, marshmallows, and candy canes. The buffet was loaded with trays of cookies, gingerbread people, and butter tarts.

Kate arrived just before seven to help with the sing-along, carrying a guitar and a bulging tote bag. She was a wisp of a thing, barely five feet tall, but she radiated vibrant energy. Her outfit included a bright red dress embellished with sparkling white snowflakes and a necklace of flashing holiday lights. Atop her russet-brown curls was a makeshift crown made of holly.

Upon spotting Rosie, she drew her into a hug. "Rosie! I feel like I know you already. Drew's talked about you so much."

"Thanks. It's great to meet you. I can't tell you what a lifesaver you've been, providing all those craft items for our Saturday events."

"I was glad to do it. I have so many supplies that Drew calls me a crafting hoarder. Speaking of my brother, is he coming tonight?"

Rosie couldn't help but smile. "He'll be here soon. He's been a huge help."

"I'm not surprised. That's the kind of guy he is." Kate gave her a conspiratorial grin. "To be honest, you've made him so happy that he enjoys doing it."

A little thrill shot through Rosie, but then she wondered how much Kate knew. Had Drew told her they were pretending, or did she think it was real? Before Rosie could ask her, Charlie rushed over and gave Kate a hug.

"You're here!" she said. "Thanks for coming to serenade us."

"My singing voice isn't the best, but my guitar skills are decent." Kate pulled a thick packet of papers from her tote bag. "I printed out a bunch of song sheets for our guests, in case they don't know the words."

"Awesome, thank you!" Charlie flipped through them. "I'm so excited! I set up my keyboard over there in the corner. I can't wait for us to jam together!"

When Rosie unlocked the doors at seven, about a dozen people streamed in. A few wore ugly Christmas sweaters, while others were casually dressed. Not as many guests as she'd hoped for, but the event had just started. She was about to check the lobby to see if anyone else was lingering out there when the sight of two familiar faces stopped her cold. Was that her mother? And her father? Though tonight's event was open to the public, she hadn't thought to mention it to her parents.

She stared in surprise as they walked into the breakfast room, followed by Jaime and Camila and then Isabella and her husband, who was carrying their daughter, Graciela, on his hip. Beside him was Drew, looking festive in a dark green sweater with a red-nosed reindeer on the front.

Mamá came over and embraced her. "Surprise, mija. We're here to crash your party!"

Rosie hugged her back, inhaling the scents of vanilla and cinnamon, which meant Mamá had started her holiday baking in earnest. "Thanks for coming. I didn't think you knew about this."

"A little birdie told us." Mamá looked back at Drew with a wink before returning her attention to Rosie. "You're looking peaked. I hope you're not working too hard."

"I'm trying not to." But all the concealer in the world couldn't hide the bags under her eyes. "Once the holidays are over, I can relax."

Or so she hoped. If she lost her job, she'd be more wound up than ever. But she wasn't going to tell her mom that.

Isabella grinned at her. "Hey, Rosie. We're here because of this guy." She pointed at Drew. "He called yesterday and gave me the lowdown. Said it might be fun if we showed up."

Drew gave Rosie a sheepish smile. "I hope that's okay. I figured you might need a few extra guests to fill up the room."

It wasn't just okay. It was incredibly thoughtful, a gesture that allowed her to include her family in her work world. "It's great. Thank you so much. I love your Rudolph sweater."

"Thanks. Gotta represent that famous reindeer, even if he's a total attention hog."

As her family headed toward the buffet table, Drew leaned over and kissed her cheek. "By the way, you look positively delectable in that dress."

On Charlie's advice, she'd swapped out her usual business attire for a crimson sweater dress and dark red pumps. The appreciative look in Drew's eyes confirmed she'd made the right decision. "Thanks. Do you want to come over tonight—after we're done here?"

"I'd love to." He lowered his voice, his breath warm in her ear. "I've been dreaming about you all day."

Even if they weren't *actually* dating, there was nothing fake about the passion they shared in the bedroom. The last time he'd come over after work, they'd both been so eager that they hadn't made it into bed. He'd taken her up against the wall, which was something she thought only happened in romance novels.

As her cheeks heated up, she pulled away and gave him a gentle nudge. "Behave yourself. My whole family is here, as well as your sister."

He scanned the room and smiled at the sight of her. "I'm going to say hi."

"Hang on. I have something for you." She fished a key out of her pocket, attached to a key chain with the hotel's logo.

"Sweet. Are we sneaking up to one of the rooms tonight?"

"No way. I'd get fired so fast. It's one of our old key chains. We replaced them all with key cards a few years ago. This is a key to my apartment. In case I end up working late, you can go there and relax if you want."

Normally, she'd never give a guy her spare key this early in a relationship because it might send out signals that she was getting too serious, too fast. But she didn't have to worry about that with Drew.

He tucked it in his pants pocket. "Thanks. If you need help cleaning up, I'm happy to stay."

"Sure. Let's see how it goes. Now, go say hi to your sister."

After he left, Rosie joined her parents, who were standing beside the heavily laden buffet table. "Help yourself. Most of the treats were made by the staff. The head of housekeeping baked those butter tarts, and I can testify they're delicious."

"Butter tarts?" her dad said. "Do you know how long it's been since I had one?"

Mamá clicked her tongue. "Easy on the sweets, mi corazón. Just take one."

Rosie showed them the carafes lined up on the table. "If you want something to drink, these three have hot chocolate, and this one has hot water for tea. Once everyone's settled, we're going to sing carols."

Mamá cast a glance around the room. "This is the same

breakfast room we visited last year, no? I don't remember it looking this nice."

"Thanks. We've had fun decking it out for Christmas." Over the past few weeks, the staff had adorned it with holiday lights, potted paperwhites, and poinsettias. One of the front desk clerks had brought in her grandma's light-up holiday village and set it along one of the window ledges. Another ledge displayed a series of gingerbread houses created by the kitchen staff. The bland room looked so cheerful that Rosie dreaded the thought of returning it to its normal state.

"You've done an awesome job," Isabella said. "Sofia told me she had a blast here."

"Thanks again for sending her," Rosie said. "She was fabulous. After she posted her videos, I got a bunch of emails inquiring about the hotel. And our last family Saturday was packed."

"That's because of your 'hot Santa.' You really lucked out with him." Isabella waggled her finger at Rosie. "I know how obsessed you are with your job, but don't let Drew get away. Make sure you hold on to him."

"Um...yeah. I wouldn't want to lose him." Rather than submit to another minute of her sister's scrutiny, Rosie scrambled for an excuse to break away. "I'd...um...better go do a quick circuit of the room. Enjoy the treats."

She left her family and strolled around the perimeter of the breakfast room, counting all the attendees. With fewer hotel guests than she'd expected, the addition of her family helped fill out the space. She went over to Charlie, who was organizing the song sheets. "How long do you think we should give people before we start caroling? I was hoping for a few more bodies."

"Twenty minutes? Give them time to mingle first. If we need more people, I could check the Gilded Lily to see if anyone's interested." Charlie gestured to Rosie's family. "It's so nice your parents came. I didn't think to invite mine."

"I didn't invite them. Drew did. Which is...um...really nice."

"He's so thoughtful. Look at him with Isabella's daughter. I'll bet he'd be a great dad."

Rosie almost didn't want to look, but when she did, her heart melted into a puddle. While Isabella and her husband loaded up on cookies, Drew was helping them out by holding Graciela. And he looked comfortable doing it.

"Shit," she muttered.

"What's wrong?" Charlie asked.

She couldn't spill her guts here—not with her family so close at hand. But if she didn't confide in someone, she might explode. "Can you come with me for a sec? It's nothing serious, but I need to talk to you alone."

When Charlie agreed, Rosie led her out of the room, hoping no one would notice if they disappeared for a few minutes. She motioned for Charlie to come into her office. Once they were inside, she shut the door behind them and leaned against it, feeling shaky on her feet.

"What's wrong?" Charlie asked. "You look flushed. Was it too hot in there? Or did you eat something nasty? The other day, I had sushi at the place down the street and—"

"It's not sushi. It's Drew." Rosie's pulse was racing, her throat closing up. "I should have known this would happen, but I convinced myself I could handle it. I mean, 'friends with benefits' is a thing, right? People do it all the time."

"Wait. Back up. Friends with *benefits*? What kind of benefits are we talking about?" Charlie stared her down. "What am I missing?"

Rosie squirmed under her friend's gaze. So far, she hadn't told any of the Damsels that she'd had sex with Drew. Not because she was ashamed but because she was still trying to sort everything out. But if she wanted Charlie's help, she couldn't keep this hidden.

"So...um...last Sunday when I helped Drew at the women's

shelter? After we came back to my place, things just sort of happened, and we ended up in bed."

"Yes." Charlie squealed. "Was it amazing? Please say it was so I can live through you vicariously."

"I don't want to overshare, but...it was glorious. He even spent the night."

If Charlie was an emoji, she would be the heart-eyes one. "I love it. So, what's the problem? If you can handle friends with benefits, then you should go for it."

"I don't think I can because now I want more than that. I want *everything*."

"In other words, a *real* relationship?"

Rosie couldn't miss the sarcasm in her friend's voice. "Yep. You were right. Go ahead and say 'I told you so' because I can't pretend anymore. I'm falling in love with him." She couldn't believe she was admitting it, but it felt good to get the words out.

"Why is that a bad thing?" Charlie asked.

"Because it's not what we agreed on. I'm breaking all the rules."

"I think you blew past the rules when you had sex. Which is totally okay. Who says things have to stay as they are?" Charlie placed her hand on Rosie's shoulder. "It's only December fourteenth. Why not enjoy your time with Drew and see how the rest of the month plays out? Isn't this agreement supposed to last until Epiphany? By then, he might feel the same way you do."

"I wish, but I don't think that's going to happen."

He'd never acted like he wanted more. But if he did, she'd be willing to work for it. Even if she'd gone into this ruse insisting she was too busy for romance, this past week had proved otherwise. With Drew, she could carve out time for her job *and* her love life.

"You don't know yet," Charlie said. "But right now, you've got more than enough to deal with. Why not take things one day at a time?"

Rosie nodded. What other choice did she have?

She couldn't push Drew. But she could at least admit the truth to herself. She was in love with him. And if she could have one wish this Christmas, it would be for him to reciprocate her feelings before their time together was over.

That wasn't too much to ask, was it?

Twenty-One

Two weeks ago, when Drew had picked up Rosie in her elf costume, he'd thought she looked sexy. But that outfit was nothing compared to tonight's dress.

She greeted him at the door wearing a figure-hugging dark green velvet gown that showed off her curves. A strand of pearls drew attention to her generous cleavage. And her hairdo was far more elaborate than the tight bun she usually wore at work. It made her look like a goddess, her hair twisted up in an elaborate arrangement, with a few soft curls framing her face.

"Damn," he said. "Rosie, you're unbelievable."

"In a good way, right?" She smoothed her hands against the side of her dress, revealing polished crimson nails.

"In the best possible way." He moved in closer and twisted a curl between his fingers. Up close, he caught the scent of her jasmine perfume. Placing a soft kiss beneath her ear, it was all he could do not to pull her tight against him. "You're utterly irresistible."

She laughed. "Well, you'll just have to resist me for now

because I'm not taking off this dress until I get the chance to display it properly."

He stepped back and let his gaze roam over her figure again. "Your dress is stunning. I'll be very careful when I remove it tonight."

Her eyes sparkled. "Is that a promise?"

"Definitely, but we'll save it for later." The thought of unwrapping her like a Christmas present filled him with a surge of desire, but he'd wait until after the wedding to act on it.

"Hang on a sec, and I'll get my things." She dashed back into her apartment and returned with a beaded black clutch and a fringed shawl.

"I parked outside but called us a ride-share. That way, we can take advantage of the open bar. The wedding's downtown, right across from the Inner Harbour." Up until now, he hadn't revealed the location for fear of her reaction.

She tugged on his tie. "As much as I love ogling you in workout gear, you look extremely hot in a suit."

"Thanks. It's my only one." He'd bought it shortly after graduating from university but rarely used it. He couldn't imagine working at a job where a suit and tie were mandatory, but dressing up for one night was a fun change of pace.

As they headed outside, she took his arm. "Are you *finally* going to tell me where this wedding reception is taking place? What's the big secret?"

"You're not going to like it."

She cursed under her breath. "You've got to be shitting me."

"Nope. The reception's being held in the ballroom of the Grand Duke."

"But Evelyn and Jared work at Northlife. How can they afford it?"

"Her parents are loaded." Even so, when he'd first received the invitation, the reception's location had come as a surprise. But Evelyn had grown up very privileged, the daughter of a wealthy real estate developer who'd given her everything except his love. Her status-conscious mother wasn't much better.

Seeing that his ride-share had arrived, he waved it over, gave his name to the driver, and helped Rosie get in.

Seated beside her, he continued explaining. "Evelyn told me she didn't want an extravagant wedding, but she's their only child, so they insisted on it. Their compromise was a small ceremony this morning, followed by tonight's big event. Sorry to put you squarely in the middle of the enemy's camp."

"It's fine, especially since I'm not paying a dime to be there."

He placed his hand on her thigh, smoothing his palm over the soft velvet. Given that the Duke was her hotel's biggest rival, he'd feared she might be irritated. But maybe she was just happy for a break from the Duchess. She'd been so busy that he'd only gotten one night with her this past week. But he hadn't complained. With three days left until Christmas, she was under pressure to fill the hotel to capacity.

The car pulled up outside the Grand Duke, which looked as imposing as ever, ablaze with thousands of white lights. On either side of the path leading to the entrance were evergreens decked out with Christmas lights, interspersed with tall pillars and giant nutcrackers. Adorning the pillars were wreaths made of bright silver and gold ornaments.

"Fuck me," Rosie muttered. "This is ostentatious as hell."

"A little over-the-top if you ask me. It's so bright you can probably see it from outer space. And those giant nutcrackers look like the stuff of nightmares."

"It's like they're trying too hard, right?" she said.

"Way too hard." Maybe he was biased, but the homespun décor at the Duchess was more his style. "It feels so corporate."

"That's because it is. Royal Host runs this place. They're a Canadian hospitality company known for managing upscale properties. I guarantee you all their five-star hotels have the exact same decorations, right down to the scary nutcrackers."

When they reached the grand ballroom, he stood motionless, taking it all in. A galaxy of twinkling white lights illuminated the ceiling, and at the center was an enormous, glittering chandelier. Around the room were more ornamental pillars and fully decorated Christmas trees. The tables were draped in crimson, each bearing a large holiday centerpiece complete with candles, holly, and poinsettias.

It brought to mind the reality show he'd been watching with Rosie—the one where people competed to spruce up their homes for the holidays—except this décor was more tasteful than the stuff he'd seen on the show. There wasn't a Santa, reindeer, or elf to be seen.

"This is...a lot," he said.

"Have you never been inside the ballroom before?" she asked.

"Never. When I was a kid, we visited the Duke's lobby once, but that was it."

He'd been eight, and his family had driven down to Victoria for the day. They'd toured the Parliament Buildings, visited Miniature World, spent hours at the Royal BC Museum, and walked through the Grand Duke's lobby. His parents had been planning to indulge in the hotel's famous High Tea, but once they saw the price, they'd left in a hurry. Instead, they'd taken him and Kate to a cozy teahouse nearby, where they'd ordered pots of Earl Grey tea and scones with clotted cream and strawberry jam. It was one of his favorite memories, belonging to a time when his parents hadn't been at war with each other.

"When I interviewed here, I got the full tour," Rosie said. "I've also been to a couple of their events."

"Do you wish you'd gotten the job?"

She shook her head. "At the time, I was gutted, but I'm glad I ended up at the Duchess. I love my team, and I wouldn't have risen as high in the ranks if I was stuck at a big corporate hotel like this one."

All the more reason she deserved to keep her job. So she could continue doing what she loved, infusing her passion and energy into making the Duchess the best hotel it could be.

Since the bride and groom had yet to arrive, most of the guests were at the bar, clustered around small high-top tables, chatting and drinking. As Drew and Rosie lined up behind an exquisitely dressed couple, he noticed the woman's ring, which contained a massive pink diamond. Definitely not his usual crowd.

Standing beside the bar was a tall, suave-looking man with dark, wavy hair and light brown skin, impeccably dressed in a tailored navy blue suit. His eyes lit up at the sight of Rosie.

"Rosalina. This is a surprise. What are you doing here?"

She beamed. "Alejandro. Are you *working* tonight?"

Drew relaxed his grip on Rosie's arm. This had to be the infamous Alejandro who'd sent all those guests to the Duchess.

Alejandro gave a dramatic sigh. "Our banquet manager is out with the flu—or so she claims—so I'm overseeing this event. You still haven't told me why you're here, querida."

Querida. Didn't that mean "dearest"? What was this guy's game? Drew scowled, feeling surprisingly possessive. "She's with me. As my date. I work with the bride and groom at Northlife Fitness."

Alejandro lowered his voice. "Between you and me, they're lucky they were able to book this ballroom on such short notice, but the bride's parents have powerful connections. Very powerful. I've heard a few stories."

Rosie smirked. "I'll bet you have. But while we're here, I want to thank you for sending all those guests our way."

"To be honest, princesa, the whole ordeal has been a nightmare, constantly having to shuffle guests around. At least your little hotel gets to benefit." He waved them away. "Now, go have fun. You're not here to work."

"You've got that right," she said. "See you later, Alejandro."

Once they reached the front of the line, Drew ordered a Moscow Mule for Rosie and a beer for himself. Other than Pepe's margaritas, he wasn't much of a cocktail guy. He ushered Rosie over to a high-top near the bar. "Do you need anything else?"

She cast her gaze toward a group of tuxedo-clad servers who were headed their way. "I'm hoping the guys in the penguin suits will pass by with trays of appetizers. I'm starving." Her eyes danced in amusement as she sipped her drink. "Is it my imagination, or did I detect a hint of jealousy from you when I was talking to Alejandro?"

"Can you blame me? The guy called you 'querida.' And 'princesa.' Those are terms of endearment, right?"

Rosie snorted. "He does that with every woman he meets. I don't mind, but Selena hates it. She thinks he's being dismissive." She smiled up at Drew. "You don't have to worry. No one here could hold a candle to you."

Her words made him feel like the luckiest guy in the room. "Thanks for coming. I'm so glad you're here with me."

"You're very welcome. Hopefully, bringing me as your date will make this reception more bearable."

"I'm way past that now. Tonight isn't about my ex—or anyone else, for that matter. It's about getting to spend an entire evening with you."

"Thanks. Sorry I've been so busy this week." She placed her hand over his. "Work has been so intense that I barely got my Christmas shopping done. Usually, I like checking out all the quirky shops on Johnson Street. Or spending hours at Munro's Books, looking for the perfect gift for my dad. Instead, I had to order everything online. I also wanted to get a Christmas tree for my apartment, but I couldn't even find the time to look for one."

He squeezed her hand. "Do you want me to find one for you? It's no problem."

"Thanks, but I wouldn't be home enough to enjoy it. I appreciate the offer, though. And I really appreciate you putting up with my insane schedule. Once the holidays let up, I'll have more free time..." She paused, her expression clouding over. "But I guess it won't matter since we'll be done fake dating by then."

The words hit him like a smack upside the head. Though he hadn't forgotten the terms of their agreement, he hadn't considered how he'd feel once it ended. How much he'd miss her friendship and support.

Did it have to end in January? Maybe they could keep up the pretense through Valentine's Day. That way, she could placate her parents for another month and wouldn't be forced to date some rando on the big day.

Rosie's voice grounded him. "Drew? You okay? You were spacing out just now."

He didn't want to bring up his idea yet. Tonight, when they were in bed together, he could suggest it.

Instead, he pivoted to another issue that was weighing him down. "I was thinking about Christmas. It looks like I won't be driving up island to see my folks this year."

"I'm sorry. That's tough, but I think you're doing the right thing. I can't believe your mom wanted you to loan her all that money."

"It's not the first time she's asked. A few years ago, I loaned them two thousand dollars, but they never paid it back." After a while, he'd stopped asking because it always led to more arguments. "Anyway, since I'm spending Christmas Eve with your family, I told Kate we'd do brunch on Christmas Day. You're welcome to join us."

"I wish, but in order to get Christmas Eve off, I said I'd come in to work the next day."

The blare of trumpets interrupted them. Standing at the front of the ballroom were two of the hotel's employees, dressed in heraldic livery of red and gold. They played a loud fanfare, capturing the attention of every guest in the room. Once they were done, the bride and groom made their grand entrance, followed by the rest of the wedding party.

Drew observed Evelyn without a hint of regret. While he couldn't deny she looked breathtaking, clad in a strapless gown bejeweled with thousands of tiny crystals, he didn't feel anything for her. No pang of anguish. No longing to be with her. Nothing.

Instead, he was immensely happy that he could spend the evening with Rosie.

Sure, their partnership had started out as a ruse—just to get him through this wedding—but it had turned into so much more. Maybe if he was lucky, she'd be willing to keep pretending for a little longer.

Twenty-Two

When Rosie had agreed to accompany Drew to Evelyn's wedding, she'd thought his primary goal was to show his coworkers that he was thriving without his ex. To prove to all of them that he'd moved on and was now involved with someone else. But as the evening went on, Rosie realized he no longer cared what anyone thought of him. He was *happy* exactly as he was.

Around his fellow trainers, he was in high spirits, joking and sharing drinks with them. When Evelyn passed by their table, he greeted her pleasantly. At that moment, Rosie no longer felt like he was using her to make his ex jealous. She felt like his *girlfriend*. Like this was a real relationship.

And she liked it. A lot.

Even if her work life was busier than ever, being around Drew didn't add to her stress. Unlike her ex, he helped her get through it. When she needed to vent about her boss or the demanding guests from the Duke, he listened to her. When she was tense, he gave her deep, soothing massages that relaxed her muscles. In bed, he was a generous and thoughtful lover.

In just about every way, he was behaving as a real boyfriend should. But back when he'd cooked up this scheme, that wasn't what he'd intended.

So what did this mean for them?

For now, it was best not to think about it. Instead, Rosie planned to enjoy her night at the Grand Duke. She had to give the hotel credit—both the appetizers and the plated dinner had been delicious. And the open bar was a delight. By now, she was slightly light-headed from the three cocktails she'd imbibed, but she wasn't ready to switch to water. As she went over to the bar to order another Moscow Mule, she ran into Bones, the manager of Northlife. He towered over her, bald and muscular, like a Canadian version of the Rock.

"Hey, Rosie," he said. "Enjoying yourself?"

"I am. Even if I'm betraying the Duchess by spending the evening here, I'm having a marvelous time."

He laughed. "I didn't think of that. Personally, I'm Team Duchess. It's been great working with your hotel."

"Thanks. The guests really appreciate getting to use your gym. Instead of crowding into a tiny, on-site workout room with a few treadmills, they get the run of your entire facility."

"It's been beneficial on our end, too. I also have to thank you for encouraging Drew to step up into management." Bones glanced over at Rosie's table, where Drew was chatting with two other trainers. "It's the right move for him."

Rosie basked in the older man's praise. "I didn't do that much —just listened and tried to support him. But I think he'll enjoy playing a bigger role in the gym's personal training program."

"I agree. He's so much happier now. Not to disparage Evelyn, but she wasn't a good match for him. With you, he's in a better place than he's been in months."

"Um...thanks." She felt awkward, knowing she was selling a lie. What would Bones think when she and Drew "broke up" in January? What excuse would Drew give? Would he blame her? Or would he just tell everyone they weren't compatible?

All of a sudden, the idea of creating a breakup story filled her with dread. She didn't want to make up some bullshit where she blamed herself *or* Drew.

Bones put his hand on her arm. "Everything all right? You look a little uncomfortable."

She forced a laugh. "I'm okay. I think I had too much to eat at dinner."

After getting her cocktail, she returned to the table and joined the conversation. She'd intended to sip her drink slowly, but her brief chat with Bones had made her uneasy, so she tossed it back quickly. As the booze rushed through her bloodstream, she crossed the line from tipsy to mildly drunk. But she welcomed the sensation. All her anxiety about the future vanished as the warm, fuzzy feelings took hold of her.

Drew reached over and stroked her cheek. "Want to dance? I've been dying to get you on the dance floor."

She clasped her hand over his, holding it against her cheek, and spoke in a whisper. "And I've been dying to get you into bed. Can we go soon?"

"Sure. Just share a few dances with me first. I want to show you off."

As she got to her feet, she wobbled, unsteady in her pumps, but Drew caught her arm.

"You okay?" he asked.

"Yeah. I should have stopped at three drinks, but it's too late now. I might need to lean on you a little." She went with him onto the dance floor and waited as the DJ cued up the next song—a romantic tune by Frank Sinatra called "The Way You Look Tonight."

Drew placed one hand on her lower back and took her hand in the other, then led her around the room, displaying polished moves worthy of *Dancing With the Stars*.

"Where did you learn to dance like this?" she asked.

"You like it? As part of my physical fitness training, I had to take a few dance classes. It's a seriously underrated form of exercise."

"I love it." The feel of his hand, pressed just at her waistline, filled her with desire. By this point in the evening, she was eager to get him alone. To shed all their formal clothing, piece by piece, and end up tangled in the sheets. But for now, it felt heavenly to be spun around the room by a partner who knew exactly what he was doing.

When the jaunty tune faded out, the DJ followed it with a *real* love song. As John Legend's "All of Me" started, Drew pulled Rosie closer, and she leaned against his chest, moving in time with him. She'd heard the song at other weddings, but it had never hit her like this. The tender verses mirrored her exact feelings for him.

She sighed and looked up at Drew. Maybe it was the cocktails, maybe it was the song, but she couldn't stop the question from tumbling out. "Does it have to end?"

"What do you mean?"

She spoke softly as she swayed against him, the fragrance of his woodsy aftershave flooding her senses. "I mean us. This. Does it have to end in January?"

When he smiled, her heart galloped like a runaway horse. Was it possible he felt the same way she did?

"I was thinking about that, too," he said. "Should we keep up the pretense until after Valentine's Day? That way, you'd be safe if your parents want to find you a date for the big day."

Just as quickly as he'd gotten her hopes up, he'd dashed them to the ground. Because he was still under the impression that all she wanted was a pretend boyfriend to placate her family. She was tempted to go along with him. If they extended things until February fifteenth, that might give him enough time to fall in love with her.

But she couldn't do it. Not when the words of the song reflected the powerful feelings in her heart. "That's not what I meant. I want to be with you for real. I...I'm in love with you."

When his body stiffened, she knew she'd gone too far.

"Rosie." His voice shook. "I'm sorry, but…"

Rather than stay and hear him out, she pulled away, fighting off a sudden wave of dizziness. It was all too much—the ballroom too crowded, the music too loud, the crush of bodies too overwhelming. She had to escape before she humiliated herself even further.

"I need some air," she said.

Stumbling, she left him and rushed over to their table. Grabbing her shawl and clutch, she made her way through the ballroom and out into the hall. She kept going until she found an exit leading to the back side of the hotel. There, she spotted an outdoor courtyard illuminated with tiny white lights. To her relief, it was empty. She plopped down on a wooden bench and rubbed her stomach in a vain attempt to stop it from churning.

Shivering, she wrapped her shawl tighter around herself. Tears sprang up in her eyes, and she grabbed a tissue from her clutch and blotted them gently, not wanting to smudge her mascara.

"Rosie?"

At the sound of Drew's voice, an ache tore at her throat. She wanted him to go away, but he sat beside her on the bench.

"Please come back inside," he said. "It's freezing out here."

"No. I…can't." She was shaking so much she could barely get the words out. "I…I just need to be alone for a few minutes. To get my head together."

He placed his hand on her knee. "I'm sorry, Rosie."

If she'd had any doubts before, she was sure of it now. He didn't share her feelings.

"It's not your fault." She wanted to sound resilient, but her trembling voice betrayed her, hinting she was on the verge of a full-blown meltdown. Over the last two months, she'd been under so much pressure, but her relationship with Drew had been the one thing giving her solace. Now, she'd ruined it. "You warned me you couldn't offer anything more."

"I know, but I shouldn't have slept with you. That was wrong."

"No, it wasn't. I'm the one who asked for it. But I should have known better." She dabbed her eyes again. "I guess I'm not capable of keeping things casual."

"That's not a bad thing. I love how you give with your whole heart. Not just to me but to the hotel, the Damsels, and everyone you care about. But..."

But he wasn't like that. God knows he'd warned her enough.

She braced her hands on the bench, trying to summon up the courage to end things. If she didn't do it now, she'd only be prolonging her misery. "I...I don't think I can do this anymore. This pretending. It's just going to make our breakup in January hurt even worse."

"Are you sure? What about Christmas Eve? What are you going to tell your family?"

She'd have to tell them it was over, which would be miserable. But playing along for another two weeks would be even harder.

"I'll figure something out, but I won't paint you as the bad guy. I can always blame my job." Mamá would nag her, as would the rest of her family, but she'd take the hit. Better that, than having them think poorly of Drew, who'd been nothing but supportive.

"Do you want me to call us a ride-share? We could talk at your place."

What was there to talk about? They weren't on the same page anymore. And if he went home with her, they'd probably end up in bed, which would muddle things even further. "I think I'll head home on my own. Sorry. I hate leaving you in the lurch."

"It's okay." His voice broke. "I'm the one who should be sorry. I wish I was capable of giving you what you want."

She looked up at him, surprised by the grief she saw in his eyes. Was it because she was ending things early? Or did he want more but couldn't take the leap? "Don't be sorry. I've had a great time. I thought November and December were going to be hell, but you made them bearable. Not just bearable but truly enjoyable. I just wanted more."

"I'll stay with you until your ride comes. Okay?"

Though she was close to tears again, she held back, not wanting him to feel any guiltier than he already did. Moving slowly so as not to upset her stomach, she walked with him to the front of the hotel and waited in the cold until her ride pulled up. She got inside the car, grateful for the warm air blasting through the vents, and stayed silent during the drive.

Once she was safely back in her apartment, she shed her formal garments and let down her hair. It cascaded around her shoulders in soft ringlets—something she'd done for Drew's benefit. Tomorrow, she'd brush it out, but she didn't have the energy to do anything now except change into her pajamas. Grabbing a bottle of water from the fridge, she sat on her couch and cried.

She let loose with huge, gulping sobs that racked her entire body. Not just for Drew but for all of it—the demanding hours she'd been working, the fear of losing her job, and the constant strain of trying to meet her boss's expectations.

But mostly for Drew and what could have been.

As Rosie's ride pulled away, Drew felt like he'd been gut punched. Had he been a fool to be so honest with her? She'd had a lot to drink, so she wasn't entirely clearheaded. Plus, they were at a wedding, which put most people in a romantic frame of mind. He could have suggested they talk about it later, when they were both sober.

Instead, he'd been painfully honest, admitting he couldn't give her what she wanted. No matter how much he cared for her, he couldn't open himself up completely.

In all fairness, he'd never misled her. Right from the start, he'd told her he couldn't give her more. He'd never lied to her or strung her along.

So why did he feel like a selfish asshole?

He made his way back into the ballroom, no longer willing to spend another minute at this wedding. He doubted anyone would care if he left, given that the evening was winding to a close. Though his table still bore signs of life—purses and jackets strung over chairs—everyone had migrated to the dance floor. Good. This way, he wouldn't have to explain why he was leaving without Rosie.

As he was heading out, he passed the table where Evelyn's parents sat. She stood beside it, chatting with them. He wanted to brush past them, but his good manners kicked in.

"Evelyn, thanks so much for inviting me, but I'm going to take off," he said. "It was a lovely reception."

She frowned and motioned him to the side, a few steps away from her parents. "Where did Rosie go?"

"She wasn't feeling well, so she left a few minutes ago."

"You didn't go with her? That's not very chivalrous."

Shame curdled in his stomach. He'd never intended to hurt Rosie, but he'd made her so upset that she'd fled the wedding without him. Not that he'd admit it to Evelyn. "It's what she wanted."

His defense sounded weak, like he didn't give a shit. Which was the exact opposite of how he felt.

Evelyn regarded him with pity. "Oh, Drew. She found out the truth, didn't she?"

"What truth?" As her parents turned to look at them, he lowered his voice. "What are you talking about?"

She blew out a huffy breath. "That you aren't capable of real emotional commitment. The last time I saw her at the gym, I almost warned her about you, but I assumed she wouldn't listen."

What the hell? He kept his voice a soft hiss, aware her parents were watching them. "That's bullshit. I was committed to you. I cared about us. In case you've forgotten, I'm not the one who cheated."

"But you never trusted me enough to give me your whole heart." She shrugged. "Not that it matters anymore. When I went back to Jared, he was more than willing to be open and vulnerable with me. To admit that he loved me, even when he wasn't sure I'd reciprocate his feelings. If you can't give Rosie the love and affection she needs, then she deserves better."

He wanted to snap at her, but what kind of a jerk would he be if he yelled at the bride? Instead, he pasted on a false smile. "I guess so. Like I said, I'm gonna take off. Have a great Christmas."

"Oh, I will, you can count on it."

Still holding his anger in check, he left, stalking out into the cold night air.

He didn't want to think about Christmas. For the first time in years, he'd been looking forward to it, eager to experience one of Rosie's favorite holiday traditions. Now, he wouldn't get to enjoy that, either.

As he pulled up his phone to order a ride, he saw a text from Rosie, sent a few minutes ago.

Rosie: Arrived home safely. Good night.

Drew: Thanks for checking in. And for being my plus-one. Good night.

He stared at the screen, wrestling with the desire to say more. If he apologized again, would she let him come over to her apartment? He hated ending things this way.

But as much as it pained him to admit it, Evelyn was right. If he couldn't give Rosie what she needed, then she was better off finding someone who could.

WHEN ROSIE WOKE ON SUNDAY MORNING, SHE COULD barely drag her body out of bed. Her head was pounding, her stomach roiling, her eyes swollen from crying. She picked up her phone, praying she'd see a brand-new message from Drew, declaring his love.

Nope.

As she got to her feet, the abrupt movement made her queasy. She rushed to the bathroom and dry heaved. After swallowing down two ibuprofen tablets with a glass of water, she glanced at her reflection. A total nightmare. Messy hair, smeared makeup, dark bags under her eyes.

How the hell was she supposed to pull herself together? She needed to be at work in less than three hours.

True, it was Sunday, but Preston had asked her to come in at noon.

When her phone pinged, she lunged for it, hoping Drew was reaching out to her. Instead, Charlie had messaged her.

> Charlie: How'd the wedding go?

> Rosie: Not good. Drew and I broke up.

As soon as she sent the message, she felt stupid. How could they break up if they hadn't been dating for real? But her friend understood completely.

> Charlie: Oh no! I'll be there in a half hour with coffee. We can talk then.

> Rosie: Thanks! You're a lifesaver.

She set down her phone, made her way to the shower, and cranked it to the hottest setting possible, standing under it until the spray turned cold. Once she was done, she put on a faded Canucks jersey and sweatpants and twisted her wet hair into a topknot. At least now she didn't feel so grungy, but she dreaded the thought of changing into her work clothes.

When a knock came at the door, she opened it and waved Charlie inside. Her friend bustled in, setting two coffees and a paper bag on the kitchen table. She pulled Rosie into a hug and held on tightly.

Rosie had thought she was done crying, but a few sobs eked out. "I'm such an idiot. I ruined everything."

Charlie gave her a squeeze and then let her go. "Before we talk, you need coffee. I got you a latte and an egg sandwich. Do you want the one with bacon or sausage?"

"Bacon, please." Rosie settled herself at the kitchen table and sipped her latte gratefully, perking up as the caffeine worked its magic.

Charlie sat across from her but waited a few minutes before speaking up. "What happened at the wedding? Did Drew do something wrong? Was he still pining for Evelyn?"

"Not in the slightest. He was completely focused on me. It was a wonderful feeling." Rosie clasped her hands over her heart. "He looked so good in a suit and tie. And get this—the reception was at the Grand Duke."

"No way!" Charlie laughed. "He never told you?"

"He was worried I'd be annoyed. But I loved waltzing in there as a guest and taking advantage of that sweet open bar." She groaned. "Though I probably enjoyed it more than I should have. If I hadn't indulged in so many cocktails, I wouldn't have lost control."

"What did you do?" Charlie unwrapped her sandwich and took a bite.

"When Drew and I were dancing, I couldn't hide my feelings any longer. I told him I was in love with him."

Charlie nodded sagely. "That's the wedding effect. All that love and romance in the air is hard to resist." She took another bite of her sandwich. "Got any mayo? This is a little dry."

"In the fridge. Can you grab me the hot sauce while you're at it?" Though Rosie's sandwich was a scrumptious mix of egg, cheddar cheese, and bacon, it needed a kick.

Charlie set the condiments on the table. "So, when you offered up your big confession, how did Drew react?"

"Not well." Rosie cringed as she recalled the scene. "To be honest, I didn't expect him to say it back. We haven't been together that long. But I was hoping he'd be open to the possibility of love. Like he'd be happy I felt this way or...be willing to take a chance on something real. But he just looked stunned. Then he apologized for not being able to give me what I wanted."

"Sorry. That sucks. It's obvious he cares about you, but he must not be ready to take that step. Could you just be friends?"

"Maybe. But not right now. It's too raw." Rosie doused more hot sauce on her sandwich. "I wish I could spend today being completely selfish. All I want to do is lounge on the couch, watch TV, and eat junk food. But I have to be at work in a few hours.'"

"Today? But it's Sunday, and you worked until four yesterday. In fact, you've gone in every day this week. I think you should take a sick day."

"I'm not sick. Just miserable."

Charlie crumpled up her sandwich wrapper and tossed it in the garbage. "Then consider it a mental health day. Seriously. You're working on Christmas Day *and* Boxing Day, right?"

"But I'm taking off Christmas Eve to be with my family."

"Big whoop. One whole day. You're entitled to take a rest day just for yourself."

"If I don't go in to the hotel, then I should head over to my parents' place. My mom always prepares her tamales for Nochebuena on the twenty-third. Usually Isabella and I help her out, but I told her I had to work." Guilt swamped over Rosie, adding to her misery. "I don't know if I can handle my family just yet. Christmas Eve's going to be bad enough."

"Then don't tell her you're staying in bed. For once, put yourself first. You've been through a lot, and you need time to recover."

Rosie was about to argue but stopped herself. Considering how wretched she felt, she wouldn't be at her best—not at work or around her family. "Okay. Thanks. I'm going to text Preston and let him know. I wish I didn't feel so guilty about taking a day off."

Charlie brightened. "I know what you can do. What about all those gift bags you bought for the hotel employees. Did you assemble them yet?"

Rosie plunked her head onto the table and groaned. "No. I have everything ready, but I forgot to put them together."

Earlier in the month, when she'd told Preston about the tradition of giving out gift bags to the staff, he'd asked her to handle it. She'd done her best, making sure each bag contained a Visa gift card, chocolates, a drink tumbler, and a handwritten note expressing her appreciation.

"Don't worry about it," Charlie said. "I can stay here and help. Since you're probably not in the mood for Christmas fare, we could watch something with lots of explosions and car chases."

"You'd do that for me?" Rosie's eyes clouded with another round of tears. "I know how much you hate action movies."

"For today, I'll put up with them. Just nothing with creepy aliens. If you need me to do a Tim Hortons run, I could do that, too. Or we can order pizza later. Whatever you need."

"How about a James Bond movie? Or one of the *Mission Impossible* flicks?"

"Door number two, please. I'll watch Tom Cruise in anything." Charlie stood up. "Come on. Let's go grab all the gift stuff, and then we can get cozy on the couch."

"Thanks." While her offer didn't ease Rosie's heartache completely, at least she wouldn't be alone. But the next few days were going to be rough.

Twenty-Four

For as long as Rosie could remember, the highlight of her holiday season was Nochebuena. Held on Christmas Eve at her parents' house, it was a festive celebration involving most of her extended family. Following a bountiful dinner filled with delicious food and plenty of gossip, everyone would pile into their cars and drive to St. Andrew's Cathedral for midnight mass. After that, they'd return home for cocoa and presents.

But last year's celebration had been more stressful than enjoyable. For whatever reason, Rosie's elderly relatives had all decided her status as an unmarried woman warranted discussion. She'd had a hard time keeping her cool when two of her great-aunts had expressed concern over her childless state ("your womb isn't getting any younger"). Or when her widowed great-uncle urged her to try dating apps and then explained how he'd used them to orchestrate a series of spicy hookups. It was more than she'd ever needed to know about his sex life.

This year, however? She'd been excited to bring Drew as her date. With him playing the role of her boyfriend, she could prove to everyone that she wasn't a dried-up old maid.

Except now she was single. *Again*. And it was her own damn fault. If she hadn't gone overboard in expressing her feelings, she and Drew would still be together—even if it was just for show. Earlier this morning, she'd been tempted to call him and ask if he'd fill the role for one more night. But she couldn't do it. No matter how much she was hurting, she needed to get through the evening on her own.

With most of her relatives set to arrive around five, she'd decided to come an hour early. This way, she could break the news to her parents and siblings first.

When she let herself in, Jaime, her dad, and Isabella's husband, Peter, were in the living room watching TV. She greeted them quickly, stopping by her dad's armchair to give him a peck on the cheek. Fortunately, the men were too engrossed in a prerecorded soccer game to comment on Drew's absence. She went into the kitchen, where Mamá, Isabella, and Jaime's wife, Camila, stood around the kitchen island. Graciela sat in a high chair, demolishing a bowl of pudding. As was typical, she'd smeared most of it on the tray in front of her, though she'd also gotten some in her hair.

After greeting them with hugs and kisses, Rosie waited for them to ask about Drew. Instead, their attention was focused on the large slow cooker at the center of the island, filled with her mom's ponche navideño—Mexican punch flavored with hibiscus, tamarind, cinnamon sticks, sugar cane, rum, and plenty of chopped-up fruit. Knowing Mamá, it had been simmering for hours. Beside it was a smaller crockpot, which probably held the nonalcoholic version.

Though it was early to start drinking, some punch might ease the tension in Rosie's shoulders. It was only a matter of time before Drew's name came up.

"Does the big one have rum in it?" she asked.

Isabella rubbed her stomach, which was the size of a small beach ball. "Of course. But I told Má she didn't use enough booze. Not that she'll let me taste-test it."

"You know it's not good for your baby," Mamá said. "Besides, if we add too much rum, no one will be able to stay awake for mass."

"If Father Joseph is doing the homily, no one will stay awake, regardless of how much they've had to drink," Isabella grumbled. "That dude is ancient."

"Maybe we'll get lucky, and Father Randy will lead the mass." Camila grinned. "He's easy on the eyes."

"Isn't he, though?" Isabella said.

"Hush, you two. Enough blasphemy." Mamá ladled a small serving of punch into a mug and handed it to Rosie. "You try it."

She took a small sip, delighting in the soothing warmth and the mingled flavors of cinnamon, cloves, and hibiscus. "It's good, but it could use a teeny bit more booze."

"You see!" Isabella said. "She agrees with me."

"Do you think it needs any more fruit?" Camila asked.

"Maybe some extra orange slices?" Rosie said. "Those are my favorite."

"Fine." Mamá plucked two oranges out of the fruit bowl and handed them to her, along with a knife and a cutting board. "You add them."

As Rosie sliced the oranges, Isabella uncapped the rum bottle and poured a hefty dose into the bowl. When she was done stirring, she took Rosie's mug and ladled out another serving. "Try it again."

Rosie sipped it. "Perfect. Now I can taste the rum, but it's not too overpowering." She divvied up the orange slices between the two bowls, then put the cutting board and knife in the dishwasher. "Má, do you need help with anything else?"

"I'm good, thanks. Where's Drew?" Mamá made a show of looking around the kitchen, as though she expected him to pop out of the pantry. "Is he coming separately?"

Damn. Rosie had hoped for a few more minutes of relaxed

conversation before facing the firing squad. "He's not coming. We...um...broke up. Two days ago."

"Already? Rosie!" There was no mistaking the accusation in Mamá's voice. "But why? He was so nice. So thoughtful. What did you do to make him leave?"

Rosie tossed back the rest of her punch, then scooped another serving into her mug. If she was going to endure her mom's questions, she might as well fortify herself. "What makes you think *I* did anything?"

"Because I know you," Mamá snapped. "You work too much. All those hours at the Duchess. Evenings and weekends. Didn't I say you're too obsessed with your job? How are you ever going to find a husband if you can't make time for anything except that hotel?"

"You need to get your priorities straight," Isabella said. "If your job is the only thing you care about, you'll never have a shot at love."

Rosie ground her teeth in frustration. "It's not just about me. Come January, my whole team could be out of work if we don't meet our boss's expectations. I don't want them to end up unemployed."

But Mamá wasn't buying it. "They're single, too, right? This is what happens when women your age let their careers take precedence over everything else. Poor Drew probably got tired of always coming in second."

Usually, Rosie let the criticism roll over her. But if it hadn't been for her mom's incessant nagging, she wouldn't have agreed to Drew's scheme in the first place. And she wouldn't be facing Christmas Eve feeling heartbroken. If she wanted her family to understand her better, she needed to be completely honest.

"Our breakup wasn't about my job," she said. "We ended things because I was done pretending."

"Pretending?" Isabella demanded. "What are you talking about?"

Rosie's face flamed as she struggled to get the words out. "My relationship with Drew...wasn't real. It was just for show."

Mamá braced her hands on the kitchen island, as though the shock had physically wounded her. "Ay, Rosalina. Why would you do that? Why lie to me and everyone else?"

Tears welled up in Rosie's eyes. She'd never meant to cause her mother grief. But now that her secret was out, she needed to explain why she'd resorted to such desperate measures.

"I'm sorry," she said. "I lied because I'm tired of all the pressure. It's bad enough that I'm struggling to keep my job, but every time I come over, you criticize me for being single. Like I'm not enough, no matter what I do, just because I haven't found a husband. It makes me feel pathetic."

"You have to admit that *pretending* to have a boyfriend is pretty pathetic," Isabella said.

Rosie glared at her. "Part of the reason I did it was to help Drew. It started because of his ex, who's also an instructor at Northlife Fitness. Back when they were dating, she cheated on him with *her* ex—who'd just gotten hired as Drew's supervisor."

"Poor Drew," Isabella said. "That had to be way humiliating."

"It gets worse. Then she got engaged to this guy and invited Drew to the wedding, along with all their coworkers. He told me about it when I ran into him at happy hour. When I mentioned how frustrated I was, constantly getting set up with dates at our family dinners, we agreed to help each other out. We pretended we were dating so that neither of us had to feel like losers at these social events. But I'm sorry I lied to you. I shouldn't have done that."

She set her mug on the table, reluctant to drink any more booze on an empty stomach. Now that she'd offered up her confession, she didn't want to double down by getting drunk. She clenched her fists, digging her nails into her palms as she waited for her mom to chastise her.

But instead of yelling, Mamá shook her head sadly. "No, *I'm* sorry, mija. I didn't realize we made you feel that way. There's nothing pathetic about being single."

What? "Then why set me up with all those different guys? Why nag me about dating?"

Mamá approached Rosie and pulled her into a hug. "Because you work too hard. You've always been that way. I admire your drive, but you need a better work-life balance. Time for yourself, time for your job, and time for a loving relationship. I thought if I could find the right person for you, then you'd realize what you were missing. That's all I wanted."

A sob choked Rosie's throat as she surrendered to her mom's embrace. All this time, when Mamá had told her, "We just want you to be happy," she'd actually meant it.

"I'm so proud of you," Mamá said. "We all are. To come this far in your career, at your age, is a blessing. But it can't be the only thing in your life."

"It's not. I have all of you. And my friends." Rosie pulled away and wiped her eyes with the back of her hand. "I'm not completely alone."

"I know, but you seemed so happy when Drew was around. Instead of just complaining about the hotel, you let us help you. We liked getting involved in your world."

"I liked it, too. I'll try to ask for help more often." Rosie let out a long, shuddering breath. Even if she and Drew weren't together, at least she'd been brave enough to tell her mom the truth. But to her surprise, Isabella was now scowling at her, arms crossed.

"What is it?" she asked. "I said I'm sorry."

"I call bullshit on the pretend thing," Isabella said. "Maybe it started out that way, but I saw how Drew looked at you. He was totally whipped."

"I agree," Camila said. "He also played Santa for your hotel. That's huge."

"And he invited us to that Friday night event with the cocoa and singing," Mamá added. "He didn't have to do that. I think he truly cares about you."

As the weight of their words sank in, Rosie was tempted to deny it. Anything to avoid confessing her unrequited love for Drew. But as she looked at the concerned faces around her, she didn't want to hide her feelings from them.

"He *does* care about me, and I feel the same way about him. But two nights ago, I told him I wanted our relationship to be real. I...said I was in love with him. He wasn't ready for that." She sniffed, trying to hold back a fresh round of tears.

Isabella handed her a tissue. "You go hard, don't you? Most people would work up to a big declaration like that, but I'll bet you just blurted it all out."

Rosie couldn't help but laugh. "You know me. Go big or go home."

"Maybe Drew needs time to take it all in," Camila said. "Men don't always express their feelings as easily as we do."

Isabella smacked her hand on the kitchen island. "They're fucking clueless is what they are. The first time I admitted to Petey that I was falling for him, he didn't take it well."

"Isabella Maria, you never told me that," Mamá said.

"Because it wasn't your problem to solve. I knew he felt the same way I did, but he had to get his head out of his ass. Only after I threatened to leave did he realize he was about to lose the best thing that ever happened to him." Isabella doled out a mug of punch from the big bowl and handed it to her mom. "Here, Má, I think you might need this."

"Dating Jaime was a true test of patience," Camila said. "He didn't have any problem saying he loved me, but he wasn't sure if he wanted to get married. That's why it took us three years to get engaged."

At that, Mamá tossed back her drink. "Well, you all know how stubborn Héctor is. Even after the doctor told him to watch his diet, he still kept sneaking sweets. Putting up with that old goat hasn't been easy."

Their show of solidarity warmed Rosie's heart. Even though her family members had found loving partners, it was good to know their relationships weren't perfect.

She wanted to believe she and Drew might have a chance. That they could carve out their own happy ending. But she couldn't forget his reaction when she'd revealed her feelings. The way he'd regarded her with a mixture of shock and pity. All because she'd told him the one thing he *didn't* want to hear.

Even so, she didn't want to disappoint her family. "Thanks. I appreciate the support. But, um...before everyone gets here..." Her phone buzzed in her pocket, sending a jolt of nerves coursing through her. Her hand trembled as she pulled it out.

Could Drew be calling to express his love for her? Would she be lucky enough to experience a Christmas miracle?

When she saw the caller ID, her heart plummeted.

It wasn't Drew. Not even close.

It was Preston.

BY THREE O'CLOCK ON CHRISTMAS EVE, NORTHLIFE Fitness was nearly empty. A few die-hards remained, squeezing in last-minute workouts before the gym closed at four. Most of Drew's regulars had opted to skip their training sessions this week. Except Hannah. She never canceled unless she was on vacation or seriously ill.

As Drew went through the motions of working with her, he tried to stay focused. Just because he felt like complete shit didn't mean he could half-ass his job. But for the past two nights, he'd barely slept. Whenever he closed his eyes, his breakup with Rosie played on a loop. The anguish in her voice when she'd accepted his decision. Her tearful face as she'd left the wedding. The agony he'd felt, wanting desperately to text her but not knowing what to say.

Worse yet, he couldn't get Evelyn's parting words out of his head. Though he agreed that Rosie deserved someone who could give her what she wanted, the thought of her with anyone else twisted his stomach into a knot.

"Drew!" Hannah set down her kettlebell with a thud. "You're drifting off again."

"Sorry. Let's move on to the shoulder press machine."

"We already did that. What's wrong with you?"

He rubbed his hand along the back of his neck. He was screwing up, big-time. How did he expect to handle his new role as the gym's fitness manager if he couldn't get through a simple training session with a longtime client?

Hannah glanced up at the big digital clock on the gym wall. "If you want to end things early, that's fine with me. I'm sure you're eager to join Rosie and her family tonight."

Yet another thing he was missing. He'd been so excited to participate in her family's Nochebuena celebration. Now, he'd be spending the evening in an empty apartment. Even his roommates had gone home to be with their families.

Rather than craft another lie, he admitted the truth. "I'm not going. Rosie and I aren't together anymore."

To his surprise, Hannah grabbed his arm and pulled him toward the padded bench near the rack of kettlebells. She sat on it and motioned for him to join her. "Sit. You need to tell me what's going on."

Even if she occasionally treated him like a grandson, he didn't feel right unloading his woes on her. But when she scowled at him, he was too intimidated to argue. He sat beside her on the bench. "There's not much to tell. Things didn't work out between us, but it's okay. We were only together for a couple of months."

She harrumphed. "So Rosie didn't mean anything to you?"

Was that what people would think when he told them about it? If so, he'd have to come up with a better way to frame their breakup. He didn't want to sound like a selfish jerk, even if he felt like one.

"No, I cared about her. A lot. But I wanted to keep things casual, and she didn't feel the same way."

"Casual." Hannah let out a snort. "Is this a millennial thing?"

Age-wise, he probably qualified as Gen Z rather than millennial, but he didn't want to contradict her.

"Your generation is missing the point," she said. "Why deprive yourself of something meaningful? Don't you want more than just a bunch of casual hookups?" From the disgusted expression on her face, she clearly wasn't a fan of the idea.

As a woman approached the kettlebell rack, Drew waited until she'd grabbed a ten-pound bell and returned to her spot on the mat before he responded to Hannah.

"I don't have a great track record with romantic relationships," he said. "Probably because my parents set a terrible example. They criticized me and my sister constantly but saved their biggest insults for each other. I spent years listening to them argue."

Talking about it brought back depressing memories of hiding out in his room and blasting his music. Anything to avoid hearing his parents' raised voices. The few times he'd tried to intervene, they'd turned on him.

"I'm sorry to hear it," Hannah said. "It sounds like they did a lot of damage."

"Yeah. They didn't hit me or anything, but it still left a mark."

"So, now you have difficulty trusting people enough to let them in?"

He was grateful she understood how he felt. "That's it exactly. My sister says I have serious trust issues. Most of my...um... relationships have been casual because it's easier that way. Less to lose, you know?" When she nodded, he forced himself to keep going. "With Evelyn, things were different. I tried to give her more of myself, but it wasn't enough and..."

"And then she left you for that low-life Jared." Hannah's voice was tinged with acid. "A snake in the grass, that one."

He couldn't help but laugh. "A total snake. So, when I got involved with Rosie, I didn't want to take that risk again."

"But you like her a lot, don't you?"

"I do. She's really special."

Right from their very first meeting, he'd wanted to know her better. Even if their initial relationship had been strictly trainer and client, he'd always enjoyed their sessions. Then, when he'd met up with her again at Pepe's and proposed his scheme, he'd liked the thought of spending more time with her. But he never imagined how much she would mean to him.

Every late-night phone call, every chat at the smoothie bar, every time he made her laugh and watched her eyes sparkle with amusement—it had all meant something. And when he'd finally gotten the chance to spend the night with her in his arms, he hadn't wanted to leave.

Hannah raised her eyebrows. "Then what's the issue? Are you afraid to trust her?"

"Maybe a little, but I want to. More than anything. I think... I'm in love with her." Up until now, he would have done his best to deny it. But Hannah's scrutiny made it impossible for him to hide his feelings.

"You *think* you're in love. Or you know it, deep down in your heart?"

Wow, she was not letting him off easy. But now that he'd admitted it, there was no doubt in his mind. "I *know* it. But I'm a damaged guy. I'm not sure I can be enough for her."

"Hmmm." She uncapped her water bottle and took a long drink. "Well, you can try, right? You don't have to be perfect. Lord knows none of us are. But if you care about someone and tell them how you feel, then that's a significant first step."

This woman was like the grandmother he'd never had. "How are you so good at this? Did you used to work as a therapist?"

"Not quite, but I taught high school for forty years. Which meant I saw my share of kids with parents like yours. Those poor kids were like the walking wounded but with their scars buried deep inside. Even so, some of them still thrived. If they can do it, so can you. You just need to have faith in yourself."

Across from them, the woman exchanged her ten-pound bell for a heavier one, then started another set of reps. Drew wondered if she was listening, but he didn't care. He was too riveted by Hannah's words. "Forty years of teaching? I'm impressed."

She barked out a laugh. "You should be. Teaching isn't for the weak. But back to you and Rosie—you might mess up, but you start by making an effort. Don't let your fears get in the way. Frank and I were married for fifty-one years before he died, and there were times when that man infuriated me with his mule-like stubbornness. But I loved him, and we made it work. I'd give anything for another hour with him."

Fuck, now she was going to make him cry. He took her hand, which was tissue-paper thin and mottled with age spots. "I'm sorry."

"It's all right. Keeping busy helps. That's why I come here three times a week. I've also got plenty of grandchildren that need my attention." After giving his hand a gentle squeeze, she stood up. "Speaking of, I should get going since I'm due to my daughter's place at four thirty. I need to change and pack up all the gifts."

He stood beside her. "Thanks for everything. I hope you have a great Christmas."

"I will. Now, as for you—before you rush back to Rosie, think about what you want. Don't fret over the future or worry that you're not enough. Focus on how you feel about her right now. Decide what you're going to tell her. And then go after her. Got it?"

Like he'd dare disagree with her? "Yes, ma'am."

"Don't call me ma'am. It makes me feel old." She patted his cheek. "One more word of advice? When you're the one who has messed up, a grand gesture never hurts."

"A grand gesture?"

"Look it up. I'll see you after the holidays. Good luck."

"Thanks." He watched her walk toward the women's locker room, slightly unnerved that he'd been schooled by a seventy-eight-year-old woman.

Even after the gym closed, he was still mulling over everything she'd told him. He thought about it on the drive home from work and then as he paced around his empty apartment. Maybe he'd be better off reverting to his old ways, back when he'd limited himself to casual hookups. No pressure, no expectations, no fear of letting anyone down.

But then he remembered all the joy he'd shared with Rosie—not just the sex but all their conversations. Snuggling together in bed, joking about the shows they watched, sharing stories and memories. He'd never met a woman who made him feel this way. Like he could trust her with his deepest secrets, and she wouldn't use them against him.

Going after her would mean baring his soul. It would mean putting his heart on the line and hoping she wouldn't break it.

But if he let her go, then he could lose her forever.

And that was the worst possibility of all.

Once again, Rosie's mom was right. Her work-life balance had gotten out of control. Case in point, she was standing behind the front desk of the Duchess on the *one day* she'd asked off.

More than once this month, she'd reminded Preston of her schedule. Even so, he'd called her four hours ago, asking her to come in for the evening. Due to illness, the front desk was short-staffed. Though Charlie had assured him that she could handle it on her own, he'd still asked Rosie to join her.

Upon leaving her parents' house, Rosie had apologized profusely to her family. To their credit, they hadn't gotten upset. Her mom hadn't uttered a word of criticism. But there had been no mistaking the sadness in her eyes.

The only upside was that Preston had promised Rosie she could have all of Christmas Day off. While his offer made her feel like less of a doormat, it wasn't as if she had any plans. Both Isabella and Jaime would be celebrating with their in-laws' families, and her parents usually spent the day relaxing. Maybe if she visited them, she could assuage her guilt and partake in a few leftovers. She was pissed she'd missed out on her mom's pork tamales.

Charlie stood beside her at the front desk, wearing a light-up necklace. "You have to snap out of this funk. Just for tonight. I know you're upset about Drew, but it's only eight o'clock, and I can't take four more hours of watching you wallow in misery."

"Sorry, but it's not just Drew. It's this whole month. Working so hard and not knowing if I'll get to stay on next year. And then wondering if I even *want* to stay."

Charlie sucked in a breath. "What do you mean? You love the Duchess."

"I do, but I can't keep up this pace. What if Preston expects this level of dedication from now on? I don't think I could handle it." For the first time ever, Rosie was afraid she wouldn't be up to the challenge.

"Maybe now's not the best time to make any huge life decisions. Not when you're in such a fragile emotional state."

Rosie nodded. Spiraling into anxiety wouldn't help her get through the evening. "You're right. It's too soon to worry about the future. For your sake, I'll try to stay cheery." She put on one of the light-up necklaces. "Is this better?"

"A little. Look on the bright side—now you don't have to come in to work tomorrow. You can sleep in and relax."

"So can you. Don't you have tomorrow off, too?"

"I do, but Christmas Day with my folks is hardly relaxing. It includes a fancy brunch at the yacht club and a formal dinner at my grandparents' house. And by formal, I'm talking suit and tie for the men and dresses for the women. For once, I'd love to lounge around in my pajamas and watch holiday movies." Charlie gave a full-body sigh. "It's also depressing, knowing another holiday season has almost come and gone, and I haven't done a damn thing to get closer to Knox."

"Admitting how you feel is a good start. Maybe next year?"

"Maybe, but I refuse to let us drown in self-pity. We need to turn up the music." Charlie adjusted the speakers, visibly brightening when "All I Want for Christmas is You" started playing. She swayed to the beat, then began singing along at full volume. With the hotel lobby empty and the cocktail lounge closed for the night, no one was around to hear them.

Rosie couldn't resist joining her. What did it matter if they looked silly? All of tonight's arrivals had already checked in. Over the past two hours, only one person had come down to the front desk, to ask about tomorrow's breakfast schedule.

But as they were crooning the last verse, a group of people came through the entrance, their coats dusted with snow. There were nine of them: two middle-aged couples and five teenagers. Four of the teens parked themselves on the plush gray couches while the adults clustered around the fireplace. One of the adults —a tall, bearded man who looked to be about fifty—approached the front desk with a teenage girl beside him. She was clad in a bright pink puffer coat and an even brighter fuchsia scarf.

Charlie turned down the music before greeting them. "Good evening, and welcome to the Duchess. Is it snowing outside? I thought it was supposed to rain!"

The man gave a weary nod. "Yep. The weather threw a wrench into our travel plans. Our layover in Calgary was only meant to last an hour, but it turned into four. And then our rental place—"

"Was a total scam," the girl said. She played with the tassels of her scarf. "Like, we got there, and it didn't exist. Which kinda makes sense because it seemed way too cheap."

The man turned to her. "It had eleven five-star reviews."

"Probably fake, Dad. A bunch of bots or whatever."

"And I'm guessing all the other hotels around here were full?" Rosie asked.

The girl shrugged. "Dunno. But my sister saw this video about the Duchess, and we told Dad we *had* to stay here."

Even if Rosie was still heartbroken about Drew, he'd done a great job as the hotel's resident Santa. "The hot Santa video?"

"Yeah, it was hilarious." The girl peered around the lobby. "I'm guessing he's not here, though?"

Charlie leaned in closer, as if sharing a secret. "I wish. He's a real cutie, isn't he? But since it's Christmas Eve, well…he might just be out delivering presents. On the upside, we still have rooms available for tonight. How many do you need?"

The man brightened. "That's such a relief. Ideally, we'd like four, but if you have fewer, we'll take those and make do. We need them for three nights. My brother and I came from Toronto to visit our parents for Christmas. We promised them we'd bring the whole brood, but our trip has been cursed so far."

"We'll do our best to improve it for you," Charlie said. "Seeing as how you'll be here through Boxing Day, you qualify for our twenty percent off special. And you're in luck because we have just four rooms left."

"What?" Breaking protocol, Rosie stared at her in amazement. "Are you serious?"

"I am. One hundred percent occupancy, baby!" Charlie fist-bumped her, then turned and grinned at the man. "You pushed us over the edge. Thank you."

She assigned rooms to the group, processed the man's payment, and handed him a stack of key cards. Meanwhile, Rosie took a photo of the computer screen as evidence the hotel was fully booked and sent it to Preston. He'd probably check his phone at some point tonight, and she wanted to make sure he knew about it.

"If you need a luggage cart, we have a few by the entrance," Charlie said. "Would you like one of us to help you out?"

"No worries," the man replied. "Between us, we have five teens who can make themselves useful."

"Take some cookies, at least," Charlie said.

Rosie brought out their last tray of Christmas cookies and handed it to the girl. "Here. You can share these with your group."

"Awesome, thanks." She took them over to the rest of her family, who set upon them like a pack of hungry wolves. By the time the group had loaded their luggage on the carts and headed toward the elevator, they were smiling and joking with each other.

As she watched them leave, Rosie reminded herself that *this* was why she'd gotten into hospitality. To help travelers make the most of their time in Victoria. To do what she could to improve their stay. Tonight, she felt as though she and Charlie had just given these families a truly memorable Christmas gift.

Once they were gone, Charlie ran to the front entrance of the hotel. "Come look! It's really snowing...and...Santa's here!"

Rosie went to join her, looking out in awe at the soft, white flakes cascading from the sky. Unlike the rest of Canada, Victoria rarely experienced the joy of a white Christmas. She could recall two or three of them. This time of year, they were more likely to get rain.

But the biggest surprise wasn't the snow. It was Santa, who was headed right for their hotel.

Could it be Drew? Or was it a guy dressed like Santa, looking for directions to an event?

Or—Holy Mary, Mother of God—was it the *real* Santa?

Get a grip. This isn't a movie. Santa isn't real.

Clearly, she'd been working way too hard.

But when Santa entered the hotel, she was ready to believe in Christmas magic. Even with a full white beard covering most of his face, Drew's twinkling brown eyes gave him away.

He placed a gloved hand over his heart. "The name is Claus. Santa Claus, to be exact. I've had a mishap with Rudolph. His nose is on the fritz, and I need a room for the night."

Rosie didn't know why he'd come to the hotel or what it meant, but the sight of him filled her with an unexpected burst of happiness. She shook her head in mock solemnity. "Sorry, there's no room at the inn."

Charlie snorted. "Now you sound like the innkeeper in a nativity play."

"Wait. Seriously?" Drew asked. "You're full?"

"Yes! Can you believe it?" When he pulled her into his arms for a hug, she pressed her body against his thick Santa suit. His lips nuzzled the top of her head, and she all but melted. She wanted to bask in the warmth of his embrace, but she forced herself to pull away. Even if she was thrilled he'd shown up, she couldn't forget their conversation at Evelyn's wedding.

An anxious flutter rolled through her stomach. She wished he didn't look so sexy in his Santa outfit. "So...what's with the suit? Did you get roped into a last-minute gig?"

He took off his hat and raked his hand through his hair, which was adorably mussed. "No. I was hoping to talk to my favorite helper elf. If she'll listen to me."

Rosie's shoulders sagged. She didn't want him to reinforce what she already knew. Not when she was starting to enjoy this mixed-up Christmas Eve.

But Charlie spoke first. "Rosie, why don't you take Drew into your office? I can handle this crowd." With a chuckle, she waved her hand around the empty lobby.

"Okay." The fact that Drew had shown up dressed like Santa had to mean something. At the very least, she could hear him out. "Let's go."

Once they reached her office, she unlocked the door and ushered him inside. As her eye caught the piles of paperwork on her desk, she remembered his naughty suggestion from before. A bloom of heat warmed her cheeks, but she forced herself to cast the memory aside. Now wasn't the time to fantasize about having sex in her office.

She leaned against her desk, placing her hands on the edge of it for support. "How did you know I was here?"

"I didn't. I was going to show up at your parents' house, but I texted Isabella first to make sure you were there. She told me that you got called into work. That's not fair."

"It's not, but I don't want to talk about it now." She was already dealing with enough guilt over abandoning Nochebuena.

The last thing she wanted was another lecture about her work-life balance.

Drew twisted the Santa hat between his hands. "Right. So… I'm sorry about Evelyn's wedding."

Not this again. "Like I said before—you don't have to apologize. I'm the one who broke the rules. Three times, as a matter of fact."

"Three times?" He cocked his head to the side. "How do you figure?"

She ticked off the items on her fingers. "First, I asked you for a kiss. Then, I asked you to take me to bed. And then, I said I was in love with you. For someone who always tries to follow the rules, I've been failing miserably."

"In all fairness, I wanted the first two as much as you did."

"But not the third, right? That's where I screwed up." As her eyes misted over, she blinked quickly, willing the tears away. This time, she wasn't going to cry.

"You didn't screw up. I did. Because everything that you're feeling? I'm feeling it, too."

She froze up, scarcely daring to breathe. "Then why did you apologize?"

"For being a coward. Even though I wanted the same thing you did, I couldn't take that leap. Trusting someone with my whole heart—even someone as wonderful as you—seemed like too much of a risk."

Rosie wanted to believe him, but she wasn't quite convinced. Two nights ago, he'd acted like he didn't want more. That wasn't something she could easily forget. "I don't know, Drew. I get that you're trying to make a grand gesture, dressing up like Santa. And on Christmas Eve, no less. But I don't want the fantasy. I want the real you."

To her surprise, he took off his beard and boots and started unbuttoning his Santa coat.

"Wh...what are you doing?" she said. "I told you we can't have sex here. Even if we did, it wouldn't change anything."

He gave her an impish smile. "I'm not propositioning you. Even if it was fun indulging in a little role-play, I don't want to hide behind the suit anymore. This is me, for better or worse." With that, he took off his Santa coat and pants, revealing a Northlife T-shirt and a pair of bike shorts.

She let out her breath in a whoosh. Having him naked would have been far too distracting. But seeing him like this, stripped of his costume with his true self fully exposed to her, thawed the ice around her heart.

"I don't understand. At Evelyn's wedding, you let me walk away. What made you change your mind?"

"I never should have let you go. That night, I barely slept because I couldn't stop thinking about you. I didn't want to lose you, but I wasn't sure what to do. Then, today, I talked it out with Hannah."

"You mean Hannah from the gym?" Tonight was getting stranger and stranger. "Isn't she, like, eighty years old?"

"Seventy-eight. But she's a fount of wisdom. She made me realize how much I was missing out by not giving us a chance." He stepped closer and stroked her cheek. "Ever since we started pretending to date, I've been so happy with you. I'd like to keep going, but I want it to be real. I'm in love with you, Rosie."

These were the words she'd been aching to hear. Even so, she couldn't quite believe this was what he wanted. "Are you sure?"

"I'm positive. But I wasn't ready to face my feelings until you were brave enough to confess yours. And honestly, the only reason I wanted to extend the pretense until Valentine's Day was to spend more time with you."

"Now you can. You've got me for as long as you want."

"I want all of it, Rosie. I want *you*."

And just like that, the last of her walls came tumbling down.

After hearing his heartfelt confession, she couldn't keep him out. Nor did she want to.

She pulled him closer until he was pressed against her. Her whole body was alive, electric with the thrill of wanting him. Wanting to taste and touch and feel him without the fear she'd be rejected again. When his hands gripped her ass, it was all she could do not to scoot onto her desk and demand he take her right now, paperwork be damned.

He pulled away with a gleam in his eye. "Didn't you say this room has a security camera?"

She laughed. "You're right. But I'm tempted to plaster some tape over it."

"If I come back to your apartment tonight, then I can make it up to you." He paused. "Or, if you don't want to miss out on midnight mass with your family, we could do that first. I packed a button-down and a pair of khakis in my duffel bag, and I'd just need to grab it from my car."

"I'm supposed to be at the front desk until twelve, which means midnight mass is out of the question. If you don't get to St. Andrew's at least an hour before the service starts, there's no chance you'll find an empty pew." Though her family wasn't known for their promptness, this was one occasion when they never showed up late.

"What about after? Do you want to go to your parents' house for hot chocolate?"

As much as she loved the idea of including him in one of her favorite family traditions, she was running out of steam. The thought of snuggling in bed with him held far more appeal. "After eight hours on my feet, I'd rather go back to my place and crash out. If you don't mind waiting, I'd love to have you join me."

"Perfect, because there's nowhere else I'd rather be."

Twenty-Seven

FOR THE NEXT FEW HOURS, DREW KEPT ROSIE AND Charlie company on Christmas Eve. Since his workout attire was a little too informal for helping them at the front desk, he fetched his gym bag and changed. Inspired by the Christmas music playing through the speakers, he busted out his favorite dance moves in the lobby. Both women joined in, making it feel like a party.

By the time he and Rosie left the hotel, the snow had coated everything in a pristine blanket of white. They stood outside the entrance in wonder, watching the flakes come down, illuminated by the streetlights.

"It's so magical," Rosie said. "Though I have to admit I'm not wild about driving in the snow. Especially at night."

"I don't mind driving. Are you okay leaving your car in the hotel's parking lot?"

"Yeah, it'll be fine because it's underground." She leaned against him, warming him with the heat of her body. "Let's go back to my place and get cozy."

"I can't wait." Not just because he was eager to get her alone but also because he had a surprise waiting for her. Which wouldn't have worked if she'd turned him away tonight. In that respect, he'd been very, very lucky.

Once they got to her apartment, he tensed up as she unlocked her door, hoping his surprise would have the desired effect. Originally, after he'd decided to find her and plead his case, he'd almost headed over to her folks' house. But when he'd learned she was stuck at work, he'd come up with a new plan. A plan he'd barely had time to put into action before getting to the Duchess just after eight.

She reached to turn on the lights but stopped short, a look of shock washing over her face. In one corner of her living room, he'd set up a six-foot-tall Christmas tree decorated with twinkling lights and ornaments. The soft glow from the lights gave the room a magical feel.

She turned to face him. "Oh my God. Did you do this?"

"Yeah. I was going to say that Santa left it for you, but I don't want to give him the credit. It's all me. I hope it's okay. I never even asked if you wanted something like this."

Now that he thought about it, maybe he'd been a bit too presumptuous, but at the wedding, Rosie had mentioned being too busy to find a Christmas tree for her place.

She threw her arms around him and crushed him in a hug. "This is one of the nicest things anyone's ever done for me. I love it."

A wave of relief washed over him. "You don't mind that I snuck into your house like a burglar to set it up?"

"Of course not. I gave you a key because I knew I could trust you. But I never expected this." She pulled away and wiped her eyes. "It's perfect. Where did you get the ornaments?"

He gave her a sheepish grin. "So...Kate told me if you shop at Michaels on Christmas Eve, all their holiday stuff is already half price. This is just a starter collection. Next year, you can add some more."

She approached the tree and held up a shiny glass ornament

that looked like a taco. "This is so cute. It makes me think of Pepe's. Ooh, and this one's a little double-decker bus."

"There's some champagne in the fridge, too, if you want to celebrate."

"Yes, please. Can you get it out? I have to take a bunch of photos so I can send them to the Damsels."

He loved how excited she was. After posing with her for a few selfies by the tree, he retrieved the champagne and poured a glass for each of them.

She sipped hers and let out a satisfied sigh. "Don't tell my parents, but as much as I adore Nochebuena, this might be one of the best Christmas Eves *ever*."

"I'm so glad it worked out, but I'm still up for anything with your family. Dinners, parties, whatever you want. As your real date."

"Don't worry, we still have our Three Kings party in January. I promise there will be lots of delicious food and plenty of festive beverages." She held up her glass. "Here's to enjoying many more holidays together."

He clinked his glass against hers. "I'll drink to that."

Though he'd taken a lot of risks tonight, he was incredibly grateful they'd paid off. Truly, this was an occasion worth celebrating.

DREW WOKE ON CHRISTMAS MORNING WITH ROSIE curled up beside him. Last night, after they'd polished off most of the champagne, he'd fully intended to lavish her with affection. To demonstrate his love with a round of delicious, toe-curling sex. But after he'd stripped down to his boxers and joined her in bed, they'd fallen asleep in each other's arms almost immediately. Just like an old married couple.

But losing out on one night of passion paled in comparison to all the nights that lay ahead of them. Nights in which he fully intended to show her how much he cared. To prove to her, without a shadow of a doubt, that their connection meant more to him than just friendship and great sex.

For the first time in years, he was truly ready for more.

Giving his whole heart wouldn't be easy. He still had trust issues to overcome. But instead of brushing them aside, he'd talk to Rosie about them. Maybe even check out that therapist Kate had mentioned.

Two months ago, he would have said he was okay with his life. That he didn't need anything to change. But he'd been wrong. And now, though he'd be facing new challenges—at work and in his relationship with Rosie—he was eager to embrace them.

When she stirred and pressed her rounded ass against his groin, he grew hard in a matter of seconds. Though he didn't want to wake her, he was aching to do more than just hold her.

As if aware of his need, she gave a lazy murmur. "Is it morning yet?"

He pushed her hair to the side and kissed the back of her neck. "Merry Christmas, Rosie."

"Merry Christmas, Drew. It's so nice having you here with me."

"Waking up with you is the best Christmas present ever." He trailed his lips to the sensitive area behind her ear and let his tongue linger there. But when he reached beneath her T-shirt to cup her breasts, she turned to face him, her dark eyes flashing with arousal.

"Not so fast," she said. "For *my* Christmas present, I want to call the shots. Are you okay with that?"

"No argument here." He lay flat on his back, enjoying the view as she stripped off her shirt and straddled him, wearing nothing but her lace panties. With the sight of her gorgeous breasts just within reach, he tried to touch them, but she swatted his hand away.

"Hands over your head. If you're a good boy, I'll let you play later. But now, I want to be in charge."

NORMALLY, ROSIE WASN'T THE TYPE TO TAKE CONTROL in the bedroom, especially since being naked made her self-conscious. But every time she and Drew had made love, he'd told her how much he appreciated her body. Little compliments and gestures that had built up her confidence. Now, she was ready to take the reins.

She tugged the covers to the side, exposing them both to the chilly morning air. Leaning down so that her breasts brushed against his broad chest, she kissed him softly, teasing his lips with the promise of more before kissing his forehead, his eyelids, and the adorable dimple in his cheek. She wanted to memorize every inch of his features. To know him in a way she never had before.

Little by little, she worked her way down, brushing her lips against his Adam's apple and his collarbone. Burying her face in his soft chest hair, she ran her tongue over each nipple before tweaking them with her teeth.

"Rosie, I want you so badly," he said.

"I know." She gave a wicked laugh. "And you'll get me. I promise. Just let me have my fun. Now, don't move your hands."

With quick fingers, she removed his boxers and tossed them to the side. Then she continued mapping his body with her lips. His taut stomach. The curve of his hip bones. His sturdy thighs. Making him groan and writhe beneath her. Still clad in her panties, she straddled him and rubbed herself against his hard length, her core aching and wet with need. Desire shot through her, and it was all she could do not to make herself come, but she wanted them to experience it together.

Easing off him, she removed her panties and grabbed a condom from the nightstand drawer. "May I put this on you?"

"Yes, but are you sure you're ready? I want you to enjoy this, too."

She unwrapped it and sheathed him, making sure to draw out the sensation. "Trust me, I'm enjoying every second." Then she lowered herself onto him, gasping as he filled her to the hilt. She rode him slowly, loving the feel of him buried deep inside her, until he begged again.

"Rosie, I need to touch you. *Please*."

She gave her hair a saucy toss. "Fine. Give me everything you've got."

With lightning speed and a touch of finesse, he flipped her over while still inside her. Once she was on her back and he was hovering above her, he gave her a wolfish smile. "Now you're going to get it, you naughty girl."

"Ooh, yes, please. Hard and fast. But—"

"Don't break the bed. I know the drill." He pumped into her. "Jesus, Rosie, you're so wet. You feel so fucking good."

She reached up to draw him nearer, relishing the feel of his muscular body pressed against hers. As he drove in deeper, she let out a throaty moan. "Keep going. I'm so close."

"I know, sweetheart." He gripped her ass tighter, squeezing it until she gasped again. "I'm gonna make it last for as long as I can."

When she looked into his eyes, she saw all of him. The man she loved, holding nothing back. She kissed him passionately, feeling a connection that went deep into her soul. His kisses were hungry and demanding, and she returned them with equal fervor.

As she neared her peak, she dug her nails into his back, bit into his shoulder, and urged him on. The rush of pleasure was sweet and intense. She held on tight, letting the sensations wash over her. "Yes, Drew. Yes."

And then he was panting, groaning, calling out her name. He gave a few more thrusts before letting his body sag against hers. She held him tight, cocooned in their little bubble, until he got up and disposed of the condom. Once he was done, he lay back down and drew her into his embrace. She rested her head on his shoulder, drawing patterns on his chest with her fingers.

"That was incredible, mi amor," she murmured.

"Mi amor? Does that mean 'my love'?"

Had she said too much? She stiffened, suddenly afraid she'd ruined their afterglow, but he ran his hand along her arm. "My Spanish is terrible, but that's what it meant, right?"

"Yes," she whispered. "I love you, Drew. Maybe it's too soon, but—"

"It's not too soon. I love you, too, mon coeur. That means 'my heart' in French. I took it all through high school."

She laughed. "I did, too, but my Spanish is a lot better than my French." She relaxed against him, sighing as he smoothed his hand over her hair. "This feels so nice. Do you have anywhere you need to be this morning?"

"I'm supposed to meet Kate for brunch at noon, if she's still up for it. Do you want to join us?"

"I'd like that. I'm so glad I don't have to work today." She raised her head to look at him as a sudden thought took hold. "But...I just realized I didn't get you anything for Christmas. And you bought me that wonderful tree."

He kissed the top of her head. "Are you kidding? You took me back last night, even after I messed up. I can't think of a better present."

She still wanted to find the perfect gift for him, but it could wait. Right now, it felt so good to snuggle beside him, content in the knowledge that they were *truly* together. Now that they'd confessed their feelings for each other, she trusted him to treat her with love and respect, and she'd do the same for him.

Blissfully happy in his arms, she'd almost drifted back to sleep when her phone rang. Though she was tempted to let it go, she sat up and grabbed it, thinking her mom might be checking in on her. She'd have to tell her family that she and Drew were back together.

For real, this time. Maybe they could go over to her parents' house tonight and snack on leftover tamales.

Once again, Preston's name showed up. She let it ring three times, sorely tempted to send it to voicemail, but her professionalism was too deeply ingrained.

Keeping her voice perky, she answered the call. "Merry Christmas, Mr. Hargreaves. I hope you're having a lovely morning."

"I'm doing well, thank you. I saw the text you sent. I'm pleased you were there to accommodate those last-minute guests. Did the Duke send them over?"

"Nope. They sought out the Duchess on their own, thanks to our videos. Then Charlie made them feel right at home. They'd had a miserable travel day, so I'm glad we could help them out. Not to mention, we filled the hotel to capacity." Maybe if she was lucky, he'd be so impressed he'd tell her that her job was secure. What a nice Christmas bonus *that* would be.

"That's excellent," he said. "The owners will be pleased. But I was actually calling to make sure you're still going in today. It would be nice if we had a manager on duty, but I can't do it since I'm spending the day with my grandparents."

What? "Um...yesterday, when you asked me to come in, you said I could have today off. In return for missing my family's big night."

"You also mentioned you didn't have plans for today. So it shouldn't be an issue."

Beside her, Drew was sitting up in bed, his brow pinched. Like he was hesitant to say anything, even though he was clearly irritated that her boss was giving her the shaft.

Drew wasn't the only one who felt that way. So did her mom, along with the rest of her family. And they were right. Though she didn't want to lose her job, she needed to stand up for herself.

Be brave. You can do this.

"I'm sorry, sir, but I made plans." Her stomach lurched, but she forced herself to keep going. "If anything major comes up today, the staff have my number. But unless they can't handle it, I'm not going in. These past two months, I've been well aware my job is on the line, so I've given up a lot of evenings and weekends. While the extra hours haven't been a huge burden, they're not sustainable in the long term. They also make me feel like you've been taking advantage of the situation."

She closed her eyes and took a deep breath. The silence was so agonizing she expected her boss to fire her immediately, but she wasn't sorry she'd spoken up. The only way she'd get a better work-life balance was if she set a few boundaries.

When he finally spoke, his voice was terse. "Very well. I expect to see you bright and early tomorrow morning for our Boxing Day kickoff."

Was he angry? Disappointed? At least he hadn't fired her outright. Nor had he demanded she come in to work today. "Thank you, sir. I'll be there at six."

When she hung up, Drew pulled her to his side and gave her a squeeze. "You okay? It didn't sound like he fired you."

"He didn't, but...he wasn't happy about it, either." She leaned against Drew, taking solace in his presence. "I'm still glad I stood up for myself. It wasn't easy."

He kissed the top of her head. "For what it's worth, I'm proud of you."

She was proud of herself, too. Even if she didn't know what the fallout would be, she felt like an enormous weight was off her shoulders. "I couldn't have done it without your support. Well, yours and my family's."

"That's because we care about you. We don't want you to lose your job, but we don't want you to be miserable, either."

"I'm not. I'm really happy."

She hadn't just gotten the day off, but she'd also taken control of her life. Instead of feeling put-upon and pathetic, she felt strangely empowered. Over the past two months, she'd accomplished a lot. She and the Damsels had done an amazing job making the Duchess shine this holiday season. She'd finally decided to set boundaries at work. She'd been honest with her family and learned how much they truly cared for her. And she'd turned a fake relationship into a real one, all because she'd been brave enough to admit her feelings.

"Do you think you'll get to stay on at the Duchess after New Year's?" Drew asked.

She couldn't say for sure yet, but she was feeling optimistic. "I think so. For now, I'm not going to worry about it. Let's just enjoy our first Christmas together."

Hopefully, it would be the first of many.

Twenty-Eight

JANUARY 11

Once again, Rosie sat in her boss's office, awaiting his verdict.

Though he'd called her in to discuss her future, she wasn't sure what his decision would be. After she'd stood up to him on Christmas Day, he'd cooled toward her a little. Less sociable chatter, fewer compliments about the efforts she'd made. But regardless of his attitude, she'd still shown up and done the work. At times, she'd felt anxious, not knowing whether she'd be let go in January, but Drew and her family had offered their full support.

No matter what he decided, she was confident she'd done a kick-ass job making the Duchess holiday-friendly. Not just her, but all the Damsels. Together, they'd increased the hotel's occupancy rate, garnered attention on social media, and bumped up its rankings on Tripadvisor, Google, and Expedia. Though they hadn't repeated their Christmas miracle of filling every room, they'd come close. Their Boxing Week special had drawn in a lot of guests, and they'd started getting bookings for spring break.

Preston turned his attention toward her. "Thanks for waiting. Before I discuss your future at the Duchess, I wanted to talk to you about the conversation we had on Christmas Day."

Oh shit, here it comes. She braced herself, gripping the arms of her chair.

"To be honest, at first, I was insulted by your accusation. I almost retaliated in anger, but I let your words sit with me." He rubbed the back of his neck. "And then I remembered that my AGM at the Devonshire accused me of the same thing. Of running him into the ground just to get the results I needed."

Rosie blinked, shocked that he'd admit this much to her. "I had no idea."

"Yes, well, whenever I've shared my Devonshire stories, I tend to take most of the credit. Which isn't true. Not by a long shot. But that's the reason the Lyons family hired me to run the Duchess. And as with the Devonshire, I promised them they'd get the results they wanted, even if it meant working my assistant manager to the bone."

Given what Rosie knew of the hospitality industry, his behavior wasn't that surprising, but his willingness to confess it took her aback.

He continued. "Because of your experience at the hotel, I leaned on you more than I should have, but I never meant to take advantage. You've done so much over the past two months, and what's more, you got your entire team on board. Instead of showing my appreciation, all I did was increase my demands. That's not the way to be a good manager. Going forward, I'll try to do better."

These were words she'd never envisioned hearing from her boss. "It's all right. Thank you, sir."

"No. Thank *you*, Rosie, for everything you've done to make the Duchess the most holiday-forward hotel in Victoria."

"It wasn't just me. My entire team pitched in, as did many of the other staff members."

"I was impressed with the way you pulled everyone together, for the good of the hotel." He shuffled a few papers together. "Back in October, when I began working here, I figured the easiest way to take over would be to start fresh with a new managerial team. Now I realize how wrong I was. Even the most experienced staff in the country wouldn't share your devotion to this hotel. You really care about the Duchess."

"We all do. I know we'll never be at the level of the Grand Duke, but I think we're more charming and down-to-earth."

"I agree. With that in mind, I hope you'll be willing to continue your role as the AGM of the Duchess."

Her relief was so palpable that she almost burst into tears. "Thank you. I'd love to stay, but I'd also like to keep my team in place."

"Yes, of course. I have no intention of letting anyone go. And I fully intend to dole out Christmas bonuses to all of you, even if they're a little late."

Thank God. She couldn't wait to tell the Damsels. Now, they could finally relax, knowing they wouldn't be facing the prospect of unemployment.

Preston cleared his throat. "However, I don't want us to rest on our laurels, so to speak. Given our success in bringing holiday cheer to the Duchess, we'll want to continue the tradition next year. I also think we could lean in to a few other holidays, like Valentine's Day or Easter. And definitely Halloween."

While his eagerness was admirable, she wanted to make sure he understood the costs. "Sounds like a great plan. We should create a master calendar to schedule all our events, and we'll need a bigger budget. Our success this season partly came about because of the staff's generosity. They baked cookies and contributed craft items, all without compensation. In the future, we want to make sure we're not asking for any unpaid labor."

Preston blanched. "Right. We can't have that. Let's set up a meeting with the head of accounting next week. Then we can make sure we have enough funds set aside."

"Excellent. The Grand Duke might boast about their High

Tea, but we could be known as Victoria's premier destination for holiday travel."

"Yes, and we'll start by focusing on Valentine's Day. We could make this the most romance-forward hotel in all of Victoria."

"Brilliant idea, sir. If there's one thing I love, it's romance."

Or rather, she did now. Ever since she and Drew had gotten back together on Christmas Eve, he'd become an integral part of her life. Most nights, he slept over at her apartment, and she cherished their mornings together, planning their days over coffee and smoothies.

Though their schedules were demanding and erratic, they always made time for cheesy action movies, delicious meals, and lots of sex. When they'd had an unexpected day off together and had been graced with unseasonably warm weather, he'd taken her hiking at Goldstream Park. She'd enjoyed it so much that she'd ordered a super-cute pair of hiking boots that she could wear for their next outdoor excursion.

On New Year's Eve, they'd gone out drinking with the Damsels, and he'd joined her family for their Three Kings Day celebration on January sixth. Though she'd had to endure a little teasing about her "fake boyfriend," everyone was glad that she and Drew had gotten back together.

"Splendid," Preston said. "I understand you're taking a romantic getaway this weekend?"

"Yes. Drew and I are spending two nights at a bed-and-breakfast up island."

"Sounds nice, though it's not the best time of year to be going on vacation. Mostly rain in the forecast."

Rosie hid a tiny smile. To be honest, she and Drew didn't care about the weather. All they wanted was a chance to get away, at a remote location where they'd be completely alone. "That's all right. It'll still be nice to take a break."

"Good. It's important to recharge your batteries. I'll be taking a week off at the end of January, but I'm going to Las Vegas for some sunshine."

"You'll get plenty of it there. I hope you have good luck at the tables." Through hotel gossip, she'd learned that Preston had a fondness for playing craps and blackjack.

She continued chatting with him for a little while longer until he dismissed her to take a call from the Lyons family.

After she left his office, she headed for the Gilded Lily. Even if it was the off-season, the cocktail lounge was nearly full, probably because they'd continued offering a happy hour between five and seven. Knox had now switched to a series of winter-themed cocktails that had proved very popular.

Clustered around the bar were Charlie, Selena, Laurel, and Drew.

Charlie leapt up to greet her. "Well? What's the word?"

"Do we still have jobs?" Selena asked.

Rosie beamed at them. "Yes. Preston agreed to keep us on. All of us."

"What a relief," Laurel said. "I didn't want to start this year with a job search."

Drew's eyes lit up with happiness. "I'm so glad. You all deserve to stay."

"But..." Rosie drew out the word. "He wants us to embrace as many holidays as we can. We're going to set up a meeting with accounting next week to review our budget."

"Make sure to toss in some money for advertising," Laurel said. "Print and online. We could draw in more people that way."

"We'll also need more money for food," Selena added. "Then we can order cookies instead of asking the staff to bake them."

Rosie nodded. "Before I tackle the budget, let's meet to figure out what we need for each major holiday. I think we can ask for a decent amount of funding, considering we increased the hotel's ranking *and* its occupancy rate." And maybe, if they were lucky, the owners would finally funnel some of the hotel's earnings into updating the rooms.

"What's our next big holiday push gonna be?" Charlie asked.

Drew grinned. "Ten bucks says it's Valentine's Day."

"Bingo," Rosie said. "You must have romance on the brain." No surprise, given that they'd shared a passionate romp in bed this morning.

Selena grimaced. "Don't start, you two. Shouldn't you be heading off for your weekend sex-capades?"

"Seriously?" Charlie said. "It's a romantic getaway, not a boink-fest. Or maybe it's both." She gave Rosie a nudge. "Get going. Next week, we can brainstorm activities for Valentine's Day."

"Perfect." Rosie regarded the Damsels with affection. She didn't know how she could have survived the past two months without them. "Once I'm back on Monday morning, we can talk it over." After giving each of them a quick hug, she took Drew's hand. "Ready to go?"

"Yep." He lowered his voice to a whisper. "I'm dying to get you alone, ma chérie."

She loved how this had become their thing—exchanging terms of endearment in French and Spanish. "Same here, mi corazón. Let's escape while we can."

As they left the hotel together, she looked back at the Damsels, who were still chatting at the bar. These were her people. This was her home away from home. And now she'd get to stay here and keep doing the job she loved.

But as much as she loved it, there was more to life than just the Duchess.

With Drew by her side, she couldn't wait to enjoy all of it.

❋

Thanks so much for reading Rosie & Drew's story! If you enjoyed *Santa Maybe*, I'd love it if you'd leave me a review.

The Duchess Hotel Series continues in 2025 with Book 2, a fall-themed, grumpy/sunshine romance featuring Charlie and Knox.

Website and Newsletter Sign-up:
carlalunabooks.com

Acknowledgments

Whenever I finish a book I've enjoyed, I always read the acknowledgments. It's like sticking around for the end credits of a movie. Sometimes, this part of the book gives me more insight into the author's process, and other times, I have fun seeing names I recognize. So, when I sit down to write mine, I try to be as thorough as possible.

If you're new to my books, thanks for taking a chance on the first story in the Duchess Hotel series. And if you're coming back after reading the Blackwood Cellars series and/or the Romancing the Ruins books, then thanks for sticking with me! I love writing, but my stories wouldn't mean nearly as much without people who want to read them.

Just like Rosie at the Duchess, I'm grateful for my awesome team of professionals. Once again, Bailey McGinn, my designer extraordinaire, did a marvelous job capturing Rosie and Drew, as well as the holiday vibe of this cover. Serena Clarke did a bang-up job with my copy edits, and Sandra Dee fixed my wayward commas with her proofreading magic.

Thanks to all my beta readers for offering feedback on the earlier versions of this book: Jennifer Rupp, Michelle McCraw, Liz Czukas, Elise Kennedy, and Brandy Shaw. I'd also like to thank Jillian Maclean, Karen Grey, and Liz Alden for helping me polish my opening chapters.

I'm lucky enough to have a community of wonderful author friends, including: Liz Lincoln, Liz Czukas, Carrie Lofty, Brandy Shaw, Natalie Caña, Lolly Rzezotarski, Virginia Small, Jennifer Motl, Lisa Minneti, Ofelia Martinez, Michelle McCraw, Kristin

Lee, and Jazz Matthews. An extra round of thanks to my long-standing critique partner, Tricia Quinnies, who helped keep me on track this summer when I was dealing with some stressful family issues.

The initial inspiration for the Duchess Hotel series came from my former boss, Byron Bluett, during one of our many work conversations. (Good thing the spice store was quiet that day!). Once I decided to write a book based around a struggling hotel, I needed to call on a few experts for help. Thanks to Kira Frommell and Cathy Radmann for giving me insight into the hospitality industry and for sharing real-life hotel stories. For the lowdown on the fitness industry, my friend Cathy Mentzer was a valuable resource since she's spent years working as a personal trainer.

Though I grew up in Victoria, B.C., I haven't lived there for years, so I went back for a visit while revising this book. Thanks to Robert Beardsell, Karen Gulliver, and Dianne Restall for making me feel so welcome during my brief stay. And a huge thanks to my sister-in-law, Julie Luna, for reading an early version of this story and giving me feedback on my Canadian content. As always, my brother, John Luna, was a wonderful source of support, especially when I needed to chat (or vent!) about the business of being creative.

Finally—pursuing a career as a writer is something I always dreamed about when I was little. Being able to focus on it now is truly a gift, and it wouldn't be possible without the love and encouragement of my family—Mike, Tasmine, and James. It seems only fitting that this book's release date is the same day as Mike's birthday, since our real-life love story is one of the reasons I believe happy endings are truly possible.

About the Author

Carla Luna writes contemporary romance with a dollop of humor and a pinch of spice. A former archaeologist, she still dreams of traveling to far-off places and channels that wanderlust into the settings of her stories. Her books have been called "escape reads," perfect for perusing during a beachside vacation, a long flight, or a relaxing weekend at the lake. In addition to being a voracious reader, she loves baking, Broadway musicals, whimsical office supplies, and pop culture podcasts.

Though she has roots in Los Angeles and Vancouver Island, she currently resides in Wisconsin with her family and her spoiled Siberian cat.

For sneak peeks, giveaways, and book recommendations, sign up for Carla Luna's newsletter:
www.carlalunabooks.com

ALSO BY CARLA LUNA

THE BLACKWOOD CELLARS SERIES

Blue Hawaiian

Broke, single, and jobless, Jess Chavez feels like the family screwup when she flies to Maui to attend her perfect sister's destination wedding. But sparks fly when Jess reconnects with her roguish ex, Connor Blackwood. A secret fling offers the perfect escape from family drama, as long as Jess can keep from falling in love again.

Red Velvet

When April Beckett's plus-one bails right before a big family wedding, her best friend, Brody Blackwood, offers to take his place. Now they have to convince everyone they're lovers—while sharing a cozy cottage in the Northwoods of Wisconsin. But what happens when the fake relationship starts to feel real?

White Wedding

When Victoria Blackwood is tasked with planning her ex's Christmas wedding, she doesn't think her life could get any worse. Until she discovers the caterer, Rafael Sanchez, is the lover she ghosted five years ago after a steamy fling in Baja. To pull off the perfect wedding, they'll need to keep things professional. But it won't be easy, not when the fire between them burns hotter than Christmas in July.

THE ROMANCING THE RUINS SERIES

Field Rules

Digging up the past takes on a whole new meaning when graduate student Olivia Sanchez is forced to team up with her ex, Rick Langston, while working at an archaeological dig in Cyprus. Given that their last fling almost led to their academic ruin, they can't afford to repeat their past mistakes. But as they work together under the scorching Mediterranean sun, the heat between them proves impossible to ignore.

Troy Story

For years, Dusty Danforth has harbored a secret crush on her best friend Stuart Carlson. Hoping to take things further, she jumps at the chance to join him on an archaeological dig at the legendary site of Troy in Turkey. But keeping the excavation on track is harder them either of them expected. Just as their long-simmering passion ignites, their boss's treacherous behavior puts the entire project in jeopardy.

Tour Wars

Sparks fly when archaeologist Emilia Flores gets stuck working alongside her infuriating nemesis, TJ Mayer, at the ancient ruins of Pompeii. Despite their fierce rivalry, they agree to co-lead a ten-day bus tour across Southern Italy to pay down their student debts. As the trip unfolds, their animosity gives way to an unexpected passion. But what happens when the tour ends and the real world steps in?

9 7 9 8 9 8 9 4 1 3 0 4 1